THE SPYING MACHINES

'I'm afraid you have no choice . . . Tomorrow's the night when the "Devil Cat" will be passing.'

The Dean Street Detectives' investigations into a series of vicious threats against a pupil at their school take an unexpected twist, and they find they have stumbled across a threat to national security. But no one is likely to believe their far-fetched story, so in a race against time the Detectives set out to foil a deceptively ruthless enemy and to destroy his unusually dangerous weapons.

A Dean Street Mystery

The Spying Machines

Bill Butler

SEVERN SH HOUSE

This title first published in hardcover format
in Great Britain 1986 by
SEVERN HOUSE PUBLISHERS LTD of
4 Brook Street, London, W1Y 1AA
by arrangement with Knight Books

British Library Cataloguing in Publication Data
Butler, William Vivian
The spying machines.
I. Title
823'.914[J]   PZ7

ISBN 0 7278 1293 9

For
Mary
with all my love
Bill

Printed and bound in Great Britain by
Anchor Brendon Ltd, Tiptree, Essex

Contents

1

The Curious Teacher

From the moment that Mr George Gorodny began to teach at Dean Street Comprehensive School, stories about him spread from class to class.

Dean Street was a very tough school, and it seemed as though Mr Gorodny was the softest, most namby-pamby teacher it had ever had. Whenever a class was troublesome, or anything like an uproar started, the stories said that he burst into tears, and started shaking all over. And soon there were quite a lot of these stories, all saying the same thing.

During his first day at Dean Street – a bright Monday in early March, halfway through the Spring term – Mr Gorodny had taught French to Classes 4A, 4B, 4C and 4D. He had apparently started sobbing in all of them – after half an hour of 4A, twenty minutes of 4B, a quarter of an hour of 4C and five minutes of 4D!

Today, Tuesday, he was due to teach 4E at 9 o'clock, 4F at 9.40 and 4G at 10.20, just before the eleven o'clock break.

The children in 4G could hardly wait.

As soon as 10.20 arrived, and the teacher taking the previous lesson had left the room, Simon Fairclough climbed on top of his desk. Like all the desks at Dean Street, it was an old-fashioned one, of wood, with rickety legs, and even a hole in the top for an inkwell.

Simon was the biggest trouble-maker in the class, and was running true to form this morning.

'As soon as Gorodny comes through that door, I'll give a signal and we'll all start shouting together,' he commanded. 'Then everyone in the front row, bang your desk-lids. Everyone in the second row, start whistling and hooting. And everyone at the back, throw something – exercise books, paper darts, whatever. I reckon we can beat 4D's record by starting him blubbing in two minutes flat!'

A lot of the children cheered, but three stayed silent – Anne and Peter Miller and Kate Murphy, who were sitting in the back row. Not that Anne Miller stayed silent for long. As soon as Simon Fairclough had jumped down from his desk, she sprang up on hers.

'Now just a minute,' she shouted. 'I don't know anything about this Mr Gorodny – nor do any of you. He may deserve everything he gets. But it sounds to me as though he's some kind of a nerve case, who cracks up when people gang up on him. And to shout and yell and throw things just to make him crack up – that sounds like bullying to me.'

'Don't be so wet,' somebody yelled. 'He's a teacher, isn't he? You can't bully teachers. Most of the ones here spend all their time bullying *us*.'

Anne tossed her long blonde hair; and her eyes, which were blue and piercing, gleamed with anger.

'Can you blame them,' she snorted, 'if we behave like that when they don't? We might at least give Gorodny a chance – and not carry on like a load of mindless hooligans the moment he puts his nose round the door!'

Her twin brother Peter shook his head sorrowfully. Anne was going too far as usual, he told himself; in fact, she was sticking her neck out a mile. Any moment, they'd be calling her a teacher's pet, and throwing exercise books and paper darts at *her* – and probably at him and Kate as well. He was already preparing to duck.

Peter was very different from his sister. He looked very much like her, but his eyes were dreamy not piercing, and he was a thinker not a doer. His instinct was to climb under a desk when there was trouble, not jump on top of it.

'Come on down, for heaven's sake!' he whispered to Anne. 'If they want to bang desks and throw things at Gorodny, let them! After what's happened to him in all the other classes, he ought to be pretty used to it by now, anyway.'

'Serves him right, I say!' Kate Murphy grunted. 'If a man goes to pieces as soon as there's an uproar in the class, what's he doing trying to be a teacher?'

Kate was Anne and Peter's adopted sister. Like them, she was twelve years old, but no one could mistake the three for triplets. Whereas Anne and Peter were fair-haired and blue-eyed, Kate had fiery red hair, and green eyes that were often fiery too. She came from a long line of battling Irish Murphys, and it showed. But there were two sides to Kate. The other side was always having strange fancies and uncanny hunches – and when this side took over, those green eyes widened, her freckled face turned pale, and she was scared of even being alone in the dark.

It was taking over now.

'On the other hand,' she said, much more softly, 'perhaps he isn't a real teacher at all.' Her eyes suddenly became very wide. 'I've – I've got a strange hunch about him . . .'

'Oh, Lord, no!' groaned Peter. With Anne standing on a desk doing her 'fearless leader' act, and Kate turning weird and having hunches, it didn't look like his sort of morning.

Simon Fairclough suddenly made things worse. Jumping on to his desk again he yelled: 'So you want us to be goody-goodies, do you, Anne? Anything to oblige. We'll be quiet as mice, then – the best class he's ever taken . . .'

'Great,' said Anne. 'I knew you'd come to see it our way.'

But Simon hadn't finished.

'– until two minutes before the end of the lesson,' he went on. 'Then, just when he thinks he's got us eating out of his hand, wham! bang! we give him everything we've got. It'll be quite a challenge – to see if, in just two minutes, we can have him sobbing and blubbering and maybe running right out of the room.'

'That's brutal!' said Anne. 'Worse than making the row when he first comes . . .'

The rest of her words were lost in boos and catcalls, as she was howled down by the class. Somebody kicked her desk so hard that she was nearly knocked off it. Someone else threw an exercise-book, which she caught and flung back with double force. Unfortunately, her aim was pretty wild. The book sailed across the classroom and only just missed the man who was coming in at the door: a mild little man with thick hornrimmed glasses, and eyes that were as round as an owl's and already watering.

Anne, hot with embarrassment, jumped down from her desk. Simon, grinning sarcastically, jumped down from his. Peter, whose ears were sharper than most people's, could hear him whispering in the front row. 'Nobody make a sound until I bang my desk-lid. Then – let him have it! Okay?'

Nobody, in fact, did make a sound as the mild little

man walked over to the teacher's desk. He made no attempt to sit down. He just stood beside it, staring at the class intently with those large, watery eyes. Finally, he said, in a thick middle-European accent: 'Good morning, boys and girls. My name is George Gorodny. I am here to teach you French, but let's not worry about that today. First of all, I think that you and I – we should get to know each other good.'

The whole class was taken aback. They had expected this odd little man to look at them fearfully, scared of yet another uproar. But instead, he was peering round the class with an expression of intense interest.

'I have heard that there are some famous children in this class,' he said. 'Young detectives who have got themselves on the front pages of all the newspapers, and who have caught many bad men, gangsters, dope fiends, murderers even.' He was getting quite excited now. 'They call themselves – what is it – the Dean Street Detectives, I think. I would like very much to meet such brilliant children. Would they stand up, please?'

Anne, Peter and Kate rose to their feet. Even Anne, who didn't blush easily, had turned crimson. Kate's cheeks were so flushed that her freckles had quite disappeared. Peter started nervously fiddling with his tie, and before he realised it, had completely undone the knot.

'Ah! So it is you three,' Mr Gorodny said, and immediately began to question them like a TV interviewer. 'Tell me, please. How did you come to be young detectives?'

'It just happened,' said Anne. 'We've been searching for clues and taking fingerprints and so on for as long as the three of us can remember.'

'It's probably because our father is a policeman,'

Peter added. 'He used to be a Detective Sergeant in Scotland Yard's Murder Squad.'

'My father was a Detective Sergeant in the Murder Squad, too,' said Kate. 'Only he and my mother were killed in a car crash when I was only four. That's when I was adopted by Peter and Anne's parents.'

Mr Gorodny nodded eagerly. He seemed to be hanging on every word the Detectives said.

'But when did you start actually catching criminals?'

'About a year ago, at our school in West Langham,' Anne told him. 'That's the place in Surrey where we used to live. We called ourselves Miller-Murphy Investigations in those days. But we didn't catch anybody much.'

'Only one stupid fat boy who hated cyclists, and let down all the tyres in the school bike shed,' said Kate. 'But then, when Mr Miller was made a Detective Superintendent, and put in charge of the Fenton CID, we all moved here – and found we were up against real villains.'

'This is a pretty tough area, you see,' explained Peter. 'The biggest crime trouble spot in London. And a lot of the crime seems to happen round this school.'

Mr Gorodny nodded again, as eagerly as before.

'Yes, yes, I see. But – forgive me – you all look so small, so slight, to be taking on vicious criminals. Don't you have a friend who helps you? I seem to remember hearing there were four Detectives at Dean Street.'

Simon Fairclough butted in. He was getting fed-up with the Detectives having all the attention.

'You bet they've got a friend,' he sneered. 'These three wouldn't be anything without their leader, Barry Bigley. He's in 5B – and one of the toughest fighters in the school.'

'Barry Bigley, eh?' Mr Gorodny took out a notebook, and scribbled down the name. 'I am taking 5B next, after the break. I will look out for him. He is your leader, you say?'

Anne opened her mouth to point out that *she* was the leader of the Detectives, and Kate was about to add that Barry Bigley wouldn't be anything without the three of *them*. In fact, he was the very same fat boy whom they'd caught letting down bicycle tyres back at West Langham. His family had moved to Fenton six months before theirs, and during his first two terms at Dean Street School, he had changed himself miraculously into a slim, tough survivor. When Anne, Peter and Kate had arrived at the school, he'd joined them, and Miller-Murphy Investigations had become the legendary Dean Street Detectives. But their success was due to all four of them working as a team . . .

Not that they had a chance to explain any of this. Simon and the rest of the class – all of whom were pretty jealous of the Detectives – started interrupting again.

'Is this a French lesson, sir, or a Dean Street Detectives lesson?' somebody jeered.

Mr Gorodny hurriedly started questioning Simon and the others about their likes, dislikes and hobbies. But his eyes no longer had that intensely interested look. The lesson got so boring that it was almost a relief when it was two minutes before the end – and Simon banged his desk-lid.

Other desk-lids immediately started banging – first one, then two, then three and finally nine or ten. Simon and half a dozen others began shouting, hissing and booing to add to the din, and someone started throwing paper darts, to add to the confusion.

'Quiet! Quiet, all of you. Please – I beg of you –

quiet!' Mr Gorodny shouted, his large eyes blazing behind his spectacles.

But as the class took no notice, and the banging and other noises continued, his eyes stopped blazing and began watering. They watered so much that within seconds it was obvious that he could barely see.

'Please – please – I *beg* you – ' he began again, and then launched into a stream of foreign words that sounded like curses. The boos and jeers grew, and turned into raucous, jeering laughter.

Anne was suddenly jumping on her desk again.

'Stop this!' she yelled. 'You've got to stop it. It's mean . . .'

'Listen to the little teacher's pet!' sneered Simon. A couple of his friends, in the row in front of the Detectives, rocked Anne's desk. Anne went flying, and landed on top of Peter. Kate stood up, the light of battle in her eyes, and hurled an exercise book at Simon.

Total chaos now reigned. Mr Gorodny, by this time totally blinded by his tears, blundered across to the door and went out, slamming it hard behind him. That slam did what all Mr Gorodny's pleading had failed to do. It produced a total silence, broken by a stunned whisper from Simon. 'We've done it. We've beaten 4A, 4B and all the other classes. In under two minutes, we drove Gorodny *right out of the room*!'

'That's not much to be proud of,' said Anne. 'The poor man's obviously ill.'

'He's more than that,' said Kate in a hollow voice, her green eyes wider than ever. 'I had a funny feeling about him before he came in, and now I'm sure I'm right. There's something weird about him . . . sinister . . . evil . . .' She was groping for the right word, and finally found it. '*Dangerous*.'

At the thought of Mr Gorodny being a danger to anyone, the whole class started laughing. But Peter did not join in. He often got annoyed by Kate's hunches, but he had a secret respect for them. Sometimes – not always by any means, but sometimes – they were uncannily accurate.

Peter's eyes narrowed. He had the best detective brain amongst them, and it was suddenly working overtime. 'He's certainly a curious teacher,' he agreed. 'Curious in more ways than one. I'd give a lot to know, for instance, why he was so very, very curious about *us*.'

2

The Fat Boy in 5B

At that moment, the bell rang for break. Anne, Peter and Kate trooped out of the classroom, and met up with Barry Bigley in the corridor.

Anne told him about the whole Gorodny episode, finishing: 'The poor man didn't have a chance. And if the same thing happens to him after the break, when he's taking your class, he's going to throw a fit, or have a nervous breakdown or something right in front of you!'

Barry just grinned. He was older than the other Detectives, being nearly thirteen, and prided himself on playing it cool whatever happened. 'So what? It should be good fun,' he murmured.

'You know perfectly well you don't mean that,' said Anne. 'You hate bullying as much as we do.' She was going to add, 'more than we do', but thought better of it. Barry wanted to forget his years as a fat boy, taunted and jeered at all day long.

'I don't like to see kids being bullied, no,' Barry said. 'But a namby-pamby twit of a teacher – that's just a little different. Still if, as you say, he's a fan of the Dean Street Detectives –'

'He may not be a fan,' said Peter. 'He just seems very curious about us. Which makes me very curious about *him*. As for Kate, she's had one of her hunches, and reckons he's –'

That started Kate groping for words again. 'Weird,' she said. 'Evil. Menacing. Dangerous.'

Barry raised an eyebrow. 'How can he be dangerous if the moment anyone bangs a desk-lid, he bursts into tears and charges out of the room?'

'Kate's talking rubbish, as usual,' Anne snapped. She had banged her knee falling off the desk, and it was still painful, putting her in a bad temper. 'I think Mr Gorodny is just a shy, gentle man who's got himself in the wrong school. He's in desperate trouble, and needs our help. *Your* help – if he's to get through the next lesson without coming apart.'

Barry smiled sarcastically.

'I see. Great. Well. Thanks very much. So all I've got to do is somehow hypnotise all the kids in 5B, so that they stay motionless and good as gold all through the next lesson. May I ask just how you reckon I'm going to do that? There happen to be forty kids in that class and most of the boys in it are skins, whom I've tangled with a good few times already. At the moment, I've got my work cut out stopping them beating the life out of poor Phil Pearson. He's the one who really wants my help. The trouble is, I can't be with him all the time, and the moment I'm out of the classroom – oh, heck. Excuse me, folks. I think it's a case of here we go again.'

Bangs, crashes, screams and shouts were coming from 5B, and Barry hurriedly made off in that direction.

'Do you think we should lend a hand?' asked Anne.

Peter shook his head. 'No, I do *not*,' he said firmly. '4Gers like us can't invade 5B, unless we're definitely asked. The whole class would gang up on us if we tried.'

The thought of forty angry 5B kids, including around

twenty skinheads, attacking them all at once made even Anne pause.

'H'm. Maybe you're right,' she said.

'Who is this Phil Pearson, anyway?' asked Kate.

'Didn't you know?' said Anne. 'He's the fat boy of 5B. He's just as dim-looking and balloon-like as Barry was, back in West Langham. And he gets jeered at and bullied all day long, just as Barry did. It's not surprising that Barry tries to help him.'

' "Tries" is the word,' said Peter softly. 'At the moment, anyway, it doesn't sound as though he's succeeding.'

They could hear Barry shouting at the top of his voice: 'Leave Phil alone, can't you? Leave him –'

The next moment, there was a yell that sounded more like Barry than Phil – and the crash of someone falling very heavily on to the floor.

'That must have been Barry,' said Peter dazedly. 'They've knocked him down.'

'There must be at least ten of them, if they have,' said Kate.

Anne wasn't going to stand there listening any more. She strode off in the direction of 5B, with Kate and a reluctant Peter following behind. When they reached 5B, and looked in at the door, they saw that Kate hadn't been exaggerating. Barry was struggling desperately underneath what looked like an army of skinheads. It was difficult to sort out the heads, arms and legs, but Peter reckoned that there were fifteen of them involved.

A very fat boy, obviously Phil Pearson, was standing on the edge of the battle zone, trying valiantly to rescue his rescuer, getting driven back by kicks and punches all the time. His large red face was uncannily like the old Barry Bigley's.

'Do something!' he yelled when he saw the Detectives. 'They'll – they'll *kill* Barry if you don't. They– they were nearly killing me . . .'

The Detectives were about to sail in when four things happened, in quick succession: the bell rang for the end of break, light, tapping footsteps sounded behind them, an angry voice shouted, 'Quick, at once, out of my way, please!' And Mr Gorodny swept past them into the room.

What happened next had to be seen to be believed. And even though they were seeing it, Peter, Anne and Kate had great difficulty believing it. The mild, namby-pamby Mr Gorodny strode up to the biggest of Barry's attackers, seized him by an arm and a leg, and hurled him halfway across the room. He did exactly the same to the skinhead underneath him, and then to the next. Within seconds, he and a dazed Barry were standing in the centre of a circle of bruised and battered skinheads, picking themselves awkwardly off the floor.

'Get to your desks, all of you!' roared Mr Gorodny. 'The Head Teacher will have the names of every boy and girl not sitting down within precisely five seconds from now! One – two – three – four . . .'

The whole class scampered to their desks. Anne, Peter and Kate equally hastily retreated from the doorway, and headed back to 4G.

Mr Gorodny peered round him at the very silent 5B.

'Good morning, boys and girls. My name is George Gorodny. I am very sorry indeed to have had to introduce myself in such a violent way. Violence is not good, not good at all. Schooldays should be happy, peaceful days, yes? It is sad – so sad when there is fighting, shooting, hitting. I *hate* all that sort of thing. Hate it, hate it, *hate* it . . .'

His eyes were watering once again; in fact, he was almost blinded with tears. But no one tried to bang a desk-lid, or make any noise at all. The whole of 5B knew now what Kate's sixth sense had told her half an hour before: that Mr Gorodny could be – dangerous . . .

He blinked hard and seemed able to see again.

'Now we must get to know each other good,' he said. 'I understand there is a very famous boy in the class. Barry Bigley of the Dean Street Detectives. Was he the boy I saw taking on fifteen others single-handed when I came in? Ah, yes. I thought so. Now tell me, Barry . . . tell me about yourself and these – Detectives . . .'

And the curious teacher went on being curious for the rest of the lesson.

3

The Impossible Whisper

Under Mr Gorodny's questioning, Barry found himself describing all the Detectives' adventures – from their battle against the vicious de Manio dope smuggling gang to their fight with the Mafia-like Fortuno mob, only a few weeks before. Out of the corners of his eyes, he could see Phil Pearson listening to him wide-eyed and often open-mouthed.

At the beginning of the lunch break, Barry was standing in the corridor, chatting to the other Detectives about the extraordinary Gorodny, when the fat boy came up to him. He was still looking dazed and awed.

'Excuse me butting in,' he said, as nervously as though he was putting his nose round the Head Teacher's door. 'But I – I wanted to thank you for trying so hard to rescue me this morning. I hope you didn't get hurt.'

Barry, in fact, was still aching all over from the battering he'd taken during that mass attack. But he never let things like that show.

'No, of course I didn't get hurt,' he lied. 'And there's no need to thank me. It was my pleasure.'

This cool act was a bit over the top for Kate. 'Your pleasure?' she said sarcastically. 'You mean you absolutely loved having all the skinheads in 5B landing on you all at once?'

'Well, to be truthful, Katie me darling, no,' Barry drawled. 'But I did enjoy having them yanked off, one by one, and hurled halfway across the room. I think I'm becoming a Gorodny fan.'

Kate shuddered.

'I'm not!' she said. 'I still think he's evil, sinister, menacing . . .'

'To skinheads, maybe,' Barry agreed. 'But he seems to be a strong supporter of the Detectives. Can't hear enough about us.'

'Ye-es,' said Peter softly. 'And I'm still wondering why. In fact, I'm still puzzling over a lot of things about him. We've just seen him wipe the floor with a load of skinheads, and silence a whole class with a single command. So why didn't he do that with us – and all the classes he took yesterday? Why has he been putting on this peculiar act when he obviously isn't really soft at all?'

'Oh, you're just making mysteries where there aren't any – as usual,' said Anne. She was fond of playing the big sister with Peter, although she was only five minutes older than he was. 'I think Mr Gorodny is a shy, nervous man who finally got pushed too far, and lost his temper. And when he loses his temper, he's quite something – almost an Incredible Hulk! But what's so mysterious about that?'

'That still doesn't explain why he should be so interested in us,' Peter said.

Anne was near to losing *her* temper. 'Well, why shouldn't he be interested in us?' she shouted. 'When all's said and done, we *are* interesting! We're – the Dean Street Detectives!'

She flung out her arms with a defiant flourish – and accidentally hit Phil Pearson full in the face. He had kept so quiet that she had forgotten he was still standing there.

'Sorry,' said Anne.

'That's – that's quite all right,' said Phil. He still made no attempt to move away. The Detectives thought they knew why. As long as he was with them, he was reasonably safe from any more attacks by tormentors. Anne, Peter and Kate were a bit irritated – they didn't want to have this fat lump hanging round them all day. Barry, though, sympathised completely. He knew only too well what it was like to be considered a freak and an easy target for any bully.

'We're off to the canteen. Want to come along?' he said.

'No. No, thank you,' said Phil, to everyone's surprise. 'I just – just wanted to ask you all something. How can someone become a client of the Dean Street Detectives?'

Anne was taken aback. She didn't want to admit that, despite their success, the Detectives had only actually had one real client in their history. 'Well,' she began. 'Since we don't charge fees, we tend to pick and choose our cases rather carefully. To be a client of ours, you have to be someone who's – er – er –'

'Facing a sinister enemy,' said Kate. 'Or a deep, dark mystery. And in urgent, really desperate need of help.'

Phil nodded. Suddenly he'd turned very pale, and looked as if he might very well be all the things they'd mentioned.

'When Barry was talking to Mr Gorodny, he said you'd had a case about a voice on a tape recorder which seemed to have come from nowhere. Is that the sort of thing you like to handle?'

'Oh, yes,' said Anne grandly. 'We're experts on voices from nowhere.'

Phil's voice became hoarse with excitement.

'Then you *will* help me, won't you?' he said. 'You see, in the middle of last night, I heard a whispering voice threatening to kill me. And there's just no way it could have come – from *anywhere*!'

Anne looked hard at Phil, then glanced round at Peter, Kate and Barry, who all nodded. After that, she didn't hesitate.

'Right,' she told Phil. 'From now on, you can consider yourself our client.'

A smile of relief spread all over Phil's face. He wasn't, Peter thought, at all the sort of fat boy that Barry had been. He didn't look bitter and resentful, intensely jealous of anyone who was thin. He was a much more open, eager type, desperately anxious to be liked. He would probably have been quite popular at any ordinary school. It was just his bad luck to have been sent to Dean Street, and end up in a class crowded with skinheads looking for someone to pick on – anyone who was a little different . . .

'Come with us while we grab some sandwiches at the canteen,' Anne said, 'and then we'll take you to our consulting room.'

Phil blinked. 'Consulting room?'

'Yes, we've got a secret one – hidden in the basement.'

'But there's nothing in the basement except the canteen – and the old boiler room.'

'That's all you know. Wait and see.'

By the time he'd waited and seen, Phil's eyes weren't just popping out of his head – they looked as though they were about to come right out on stalks. After they'd collected their sandwiches, the Detectives led him through a maze of passages into a part of the basement he had never dreamed existed. Dean Street School was an old building, originally erected as a reform school for boys early in Queen Victoria's reign. The basement was a rabbit-warren of rooms that had once been the servants' quarters. The school had converted the biggest of these rooms – the old kitchen – into a canteen, and used a few more of them for storage; but the rest had long ago been closed off. As a result, there was quite a large area of the basement, containing old pantries, sculleries and laundering-rooms where nobody went from one end of the year to the other – except spiders, cockroaches, scampering mice and the Dean Street Detectives.

Phil found himself being led down a long, dark, draughty corridor, with dust and cobwebs everywhere.

'We call this the Corridor of Ghosts,' Kate told him in a scared whisper. 'I don't like to hang about here much myself.'

'Neither do any of us,' Barry admitted. 'Kate starts screaming if we do. And if you ever hear a real Kate Murphy scream, your eardrums are never the same again.'

Anne opened a door on the right. 'Here we are,' she said, proudly. 'Our secret consulting room. And it *is* secret, too. There's no one for miles around to hear anything we say.'

'Some rival school detectives had the cheek to set up

a consulting room next door to us a while ago,' said Kate. 'But they seemed to have packed it in now. We haven't seen a sign of them for weeks.'

They ushered Phil into the room. He stared round it, blinking dazedly. The place had once been a servants' headquarters, and high on one wall were rusty old bells, labelled HEADMASTER'S STUDY, MASTER'S COMMON ROOM, and so on. Another wall contained a notice-board, covered with the Detectives' press-cuttings. These included whole front pages from the *Sun*, the *Daily Star* and the *Daily Mirror*, with headlines like: TWELVE-YEAR-OLD SHERLOCKS SMASH KILLER GANG. Another wall featured a CID wallchart on how to make Identikit pictures, and the fourth had an old film poster on it, advertising Humphrey Bogart in *The Big Sleep*. There was quite a lot of furniture – of sorts: two battered leather armchairs; an old linen chest, full of things like magnifying glasses and fingerprint powders, and a small table containing mugs, glasses and cans of Coke. There was also a tape-recorder and mike.

Anne waved Phil towards one of the leather armchairs. Still munching their sandwiches, the Detectives settled down to listen to his story. Peter flung himself into the other leather armchair, leant back and narrowed his eyes, for all the world like a twelve-year-old Sherlock Holmes. Kate sat on one of the arms of the same chair. Anne perched herself on the linen chest, and started handing out Coke. Barry lounged against the wall in front of the Bogart poster.

'Well. Get on with it,' said Anne impatiently, as she handed Phil a mug.

'And if you don't know where to start,' said Peter,

'I'll tell you. Just where were you when you heard this strange whisper?'

'In the bathroom,' said Phil. 'I'd gone to get a drink of water.'

'What – in the middle of the night?' asked Kate.

'Yes. I'd woken up thirsty.'

'Okay. So you went across to the bathroom. And then – '

'I was just about to turn the tap on, when I heard the whisper. It was loud and clear, and seemed to come from right beside me. Yet I had the light on, and could see that there was nothing and nobody in that bathroom but me.'

'What did the whisper say?' Peter asked.

Phil took a sip of Coke before replying. That was a mistake. He choked over it, and jumped out of the armchair, coughing and spluttering. His face was suddenly crimson and balloon-like, reminding Peter, Anne and Kate once again of the old Barry Bigley. Perhaps it reminded Barry of himself. He shuffled his feet uncomfortably, and snapped at Phil.

'Well, go on. What *did* the whisper say?'

Phil slumped back in the armchair. His face was still crimson, and now it was covered with sweat.

'It – it was a very frightening voice, with a foreign accent. It started by saying: "*I'm afraid you have no choice, Pearson. Tomorrow's the night when the something –* " I couldn't catch what "*–will be passing. You must let the rest of the machines in by then.*" '

'The rest of the machines?' said the Detectives together. They were looking almost as bewildered as Phil himself.

'That's right,' Phil said. 'And then it began making threats. "*If you don't, some very nasty things will happen to you and all your family,*" it said. "*Some very nasty things indeed.*" I came out of that bathroom shaking all over – like – like I am now.'

'Phew!' said Kate. 'I don't blame you.'

Anne was sterner.

'Have some more Coke, and pull yourself together,' she commanded.

'Careful, or you'll start him choking again,' said Kate.

Peter, his eyes wide-open for once, was leaning forward in his chair. 'Tomorrow's the night when what will be passing?' he asked softly. 'If only you'd caught that missing word.'

'It was two words, I think,' Phil said. 'And I can tell you what they sounded like, although you'll probably think me crazy.'

'Crazy or not, we'll buy it,' said Peter. 'What *did* they sound like?'

Phil stared round at the Detectives, the sweat now pouring down his forehead.

'Devil cat,' he said.

4

Detective at Work

It was Kate's turn to choke over her drink.

'Let's get this – this straight,' she spluttered. 'The whisper told you that you must let the rest of the machines in, because tomorrow's the night when the Devil Cat will be passing. But what the – devil cat can that possibly mean?'

'Don't ask me,' said Phil. 'I just can't make any sense of it at all. Any more than I can figure out where on earth the whisper came from! I've told you there was no one in the bathroom. Well, there was no one in the toilet either – that's next door to the bathroom – or on the landing. I went back to bed terrified, wondering if I'd dreamed it all.'

'Well, that is a possible answer,' said Anne.

'No, it isn't,' said Phil, almost angrily. 'I know I was awake. I even pinched myself to make sure. So hard that it left this bruise . . . ' He rolled up his sleeve and showed her a nasty blue pinch-mark on his podgy arm.

Anne winced at the sight of it.

'Okay,' she said hastily. 'So you weren't dreaming.'

There was a pause. Everyone seemed to be so puzzled that they'd run out of questions – except for Peter, who was just getting into his stride as the star detective of the group. He was doing the full Sherlock

Holmes bit now – leaning back and pressing his finger-tips together like the great man himself.

'What time was all this?' he asked suddenly.

Phil shook his head. 'I haven't got a watch, so I've no idea. But it couldn't have been all that late, because about a minute afterwards, I heard the back door open, and then my father came up and went to bed.'

'And your mother – where was she all this time?'

'She was in bed, fast asleep. I passed the door of Mum and Dad's room on the way to the bathroom. The door was open, and I heard her heavy breathing, as a matter of fact, she was almost snoring.'

'Does your father often come home late?'

'No. Hardly ever. But last night, he had to go to some meeting. I remember hearing him telling Mum not to lock up.'

Anne finally thought of a question – to her great relief. She never let Peter have all the limelight, if she could help it.

'What does your father do?' she asked.

Phil found it hard to explain.

'Well – he's got a funny sort of job. You know there are a lot of warehouses around here.'

The Detectives nodded. There were times when it seemed as if Fenton consisted of nothing but miles of empty factories and warehouses. They cycled past hundreds of them every day on their way to and from school.

'Yes,' said Barry sarcastically. 'We had gathered that.'

'Well, most of the warehouses have closed down because the firms that owned them went bust. But one or two firms aren't completely finished. They've just closed their warehouses for the time being, and hope to open them again when business picks up. One of these firms – Benholt Plastic Mouldings – owns about five warehouses, all on the same piece of land in Rochester Road. And they've made my father caretaker and maintenance man in charge of them. He has to make sure they stay in good condition and don't fall apart. He wanders round them all the time, mending hinges, painting doors and things like that. He used to have his own decorating business, so the job is right up his street. What's the matter? What have I said?'

Peter had come bounding out of his armchair. He was no longer putting on any sort of an act. He was really being a detective at work. His eyes were gleaming, and for once, they were almost as piercing as Anne's.

'Listen,' he said. 'It's pretty obvious what's going on. Someone wants some equipment moved into those warehouses and is threatening your father. Obviously, he came back with your father from the meeting, and whispered that threat, just as your father was about to let himself in by the back door. If your house is like ours, there's a drain near that door, with pipes leading up to the bathroom. Sounds can travel up the pipe, and out into the bath and the bathroom basin. When I've been taking a shower or having a bath, I've often accidentally overheard things my mother was saying to a neighbour over the fence. Annoying things, sometimes – like, "That son of mine is getting dreamier and sillier every day"!'

'Well, you are, dear brother,' said Anne. 'But I've got to admit you're not being dreamy or silly now. That was absolutely brilliant. It's taken my breath away.'

Praise from Anne was so rare that it took *Peter's* breath away. He soon recovered, though, and began prowling round the room, firing off questions at machine-gun rate.

'But why should a gang of villains want to install machines in a lot of old warehouses? What sort of machines could they be? And why do the rest of them have to be in by tomorrow night?'

'We know that, anyway,' said Kate. 'It's because the Devil Cat's passing!' Her wild Irish imagination took over. 'Hey! Supposing they're a black magic gang – a coven of witches who want the warehouses to practise strange, evil ceremonies to avoid the Curse of the Devil Cat!'

Barry groaned.

'Heaven preserve us from the Curse of the Stupid Kate!' he murmured. 'If they were devil-worshippers, what would they want machines for? It's much more likely that they're a gang of bank-robbers, who need the warehouses to store their getaway vans.'

'That doesn't fit either,' said Peter, shaking his head. 'Getaway van-drivers don't need machines any more than devil-worshippers. And don't forget, the gang wants that equipment in because tomorrow night, something's *passing*. A bank isn't going to come trundling past those warehouses on wheels.'

'Then what *is*?' asked Anne.

'Search me,' said Peter. 'But I reckon it's something the gang wants to ambush – or attack.'

That started Kate's imagination working again.

'A lorry load of bullion from the Bank of England– worth millions and millions of pounds . . .'

She almost expected everyone to laugh at her, and was quite startled when nobody did.

'It could very well be something like that,' Peter agreed. 'It's got to be something pretty big anyway – because a lot of equipment's wanted. Some of the machines are in the warehouse already, remember. And the rest Phil's father's got to let in tonight – or else.'

Phil hadn't said anything for a long time. Suddenly he couldn't stop talking.

'Or else they're going to murder him . . . and Mum . . . and me,' he gulped. 'Poor Dad. No wonder he's been looking as white as a sheet for weeks. Mum thought he was ill – kept wanting him to go to the doctor. He has a weak heart already. This – this could kill him.' His face turned abruptly from crimson to white. 'And if he does what he's told – just says nothing and lets them bring in this equipment – then the police could arrest him for being mixed up in a million-pound bullion raid or something! And that would *definitely* kill him. You've . . . you've got to help me . . .'

Anne, who was never brusque with anyone who appealed to her beloved Detectives for rescue, struck just the right firm and reassuring note.

'Don't worry,' she told him. 'Of course we've got to help you. You're our client! And I know just how we're going to start.' She turned to the others. 'First, we've got to check that Peter's theory is right. That means going to the warehouses, and seeing for ourselves if some machines have been moved in there – and what they are. Agreed?'

'Hold on,' said Peter. 'Those warehouses will be locked up, and we'll never get in.'

'Unless,' said Barry, looking hard at Phil, 'you know where your Dad keeps the keys, and could get hold of them.'

'I – I think I could do that,' Phil said. 'Dad usually keeps them in his overcoat pocket. And when he comes home in the evening, he always hangs the coat up in the hall. I don't want to pick his pocket, but – but if it's to help save his life . . .'

He broke off, confused and dazed. At any moment, he looked as if he might start pinching himself again, to make sure he wasn't having a nightmare. Peter didn't help by saying:

'There's one thing I ought to mention. If these machines are valuable, the villains could have put a guard on them. In which case, we could be heading straight into trouble. Big trouble.'

'Oh, we're always heading into trouble, according to you,' said Anne. 'If we waited until you thought everything was safe, we'd be hanging about until the cows came home.'

'Or until all the Devil Cats had passed,' murmured Barry.

'Exactly,' said Anne. 'Right then. We'll meet outside the warehouse at eight.' And she ended the meeting with her favourite words: 'Let's go!'

The Detectives went out of the consulting room laughing. Phil felt more dazed than ever. But he was not only dazed now; he was envious. He wanted more than anything to be like one of these slim, seemingly fearless Detectives. But what hope was there of that?

Could anyone imagine a stupid fat boy turning into someone like Barry Bigley, he asked himself bitterly, as he followed the Detectives down the dusty corridor and up into the main school building.

5

Through the Wire

The time, by Anne's four-dial digital watch, was 8.34 and 27 seconds precisely. And thirty-four minutes and twenty-seven seconds was quite long enough, in her opinion, to wait for a fat idiot like Phil Pearson.

A cold March wind was blowing down Rochester Road, and the Detectives felt frozen stiff. They were also very cramped. The road, one of the A routes to the North, was one of the few places in Fenton that was brilliantly lit at night: the lamp-posts, giving out a weird orange sodium vapour light, were far too high to be smashed by vandals. Because of all this light, the Detectives had thought it wise to keep hidden, and had spent the past half hour crouching behind a rusty metal sign advertising Benholt Plastic Mouldings, about twenty metres past the main warehouse gate.

It wasn't the world's best hiding-place. The wind kept catching the sign, and had twice nearly blown it over on top of the Detectives. And all the time, it had blown *round* it, whistling past their ears and through their hair, numbing their noses and fingers. In all that time, they hadn't seen the slightest sign of a villain keeping guard on the place. In fact, they hadn't seen a living soul – apart from the drivers of the endless stream of cars and lorries roaring by, and each of them had been glimpsed for a split-second only. There was nothing to stop or slow down for in Rochester Road.

The place was simply a desert of closed factories and empty warehouses, stretching in either direction as far as the eye could see. It was like being in the middle of a ghost town, made all the more eerie by the unearthly orange light.

Anne took one more look at her watch – it said 8.34 and 30 seconds now – and then stood up abruptly, nearly knocking the metal sign over.

'Well, that's it,' she said. 'We're not hanging about for Phil one second longer. Something must have happened to him.'

'What can have happened?' asked Kate.

'Lots of things,' said Peter. 'His father may not have come home yet. Or perhaps he's come home, but not hung his coat up. Or maybe the keys didn't turn out to be in its pocket . . .'

'We can soon find out, anyway,' said Anne. 'There's a phone box over there. And I remembered to get Phil's number, along with his name and address. I'm keeping a Dean Street Detectives notebook, with full particulars of every client, past and present.'

'What, both of them?' murmured Barry.

Anne ignored that, and led the way to the telephone kiosk.

'Let's hope vandals haven't got to it before us,' said Peter.

They had. Every pane of glass in the kiosk had been smashed, and crude messages had been chalked and sprayed all over the walls. But by some miracle, the telephone itself still worked, and so did the coin box.

Anne dialled the number, and a man's voice snapped: 'Hell*o*, hell*o*.' He sounded very irritable or very nervous – perhaps both.

Anne put a coin into the box, and then asked: 'Can we speak to Phil, please?'

'No, you certainly can't,' said the voice. It started talking in furious, jerky sentences. 'He's been taken ill. Flu, I think. Red as a beetroot. High temperature. Made him go straight to bed. *Straight* to bed.'

'Is that Mr Pearson?' Anne asked, though it was pretty obvious that it was.

'Yes. That's right. His father. I suppose you're one of the children he was going out with tonight. Well, I'm to tell you he's very sorry, but he won't be coming. He wanted to come, in spite of his condition, but his mother and I wouldn't hear of it. Wouldn't hear of it *at all*! It'd be madness for him to come out in that state – madness . . .'

The rest of the words were lost in crackles, as the vandalised phone gave up.

Anne hung up the receiver, shivering. The wind whistling through the glassless kiosk was even more piercing than it had been round that metal sign. She repeated the words to the others, adding: 'There's something weird about all this. Phil didn't look at all ill at lunch time.'

'Didn't he?' Peter said. 'The way he kept turning red and sweating, I thought he looked scared sick.'

'They're quite a family,' said Anne. 'That's the way the father sounds *now*!'

Peter frowned.

'Hey. Do you suppose Mr Pearson caught Phil stealing the keys, and made him tell the whole story? In that case, he might have locked him in and is just pretending he's ill.'

Anne was in no mood for Peter's theories now.

'Who knows? And what does it matter, anyway? The main point is – we're stuck. We can't get into the warehouses without those keys. We can't keep watch outside the main gates much longer without Mum and

Dad going bananas when we get home. In any case, the villains probably won't be moving in "the rest of the machines", whatever that means, till the middle of the night.'

'Right. Then let's pack it in and get out of here!' said Kate. She still felt frozen – and an eerie ghost town complete with whistling winds was definitely not the sort of place to appeal to Kate.

'That seems a good idea to me,' said Peter.

'It *would*!' said Anne scornfully. There was nothing she hated more than giving up.

As the Detectives walked over to their bikes, which they'd hidden in a patch of scrubland close by the metal sign, she stopped and took one more look back at the main gate.

It was a rusty metal structure, firmly padlocked, set in a tall fence of steel mesh which went right round the grounds. As far as she could see, there were no holes in the mesh anywhere; even a rat or a mouse would have had trouble breaking through.

'If only,' she mused, 'one of us had thought to bring – '

'A pair of wire-cutting pliers?' came Barry's mocking voice in her ear. 'Well, now, isn't that a coincidence? A Dean Street Detective must always be prepared, I told myself, and I happened to pop that very thing into my saddlebag.'

Kate groaned. Peter sighed. Anne stared.

'Why didn't you say so before?'

'If you want the truth,' said Barry, 'I've been screwing up the nerve to use them. There's a risk that that fence is wired up to an alarm system. In which case, one clip and all hell will break loose. But if you reckon we should chance it, O fearless leader – '

'I certainly do,' said Anne. 'There's nobody around

to take any notice if the alarm *does* go off!'

'Unless,' said Peter, 'there are some villains hiding inside, guarding these mysterious machines. They'll take notice, all right. They're liable to come at us with all guns blazing.'

But there was no stopping Anne now.

'I'll come at you with all guns blazing in a minute,' she said. 'Get on with it, Barry, for Heaven's sake.'

They had reached the piece of scrubland now. Barry stooped over his bike, and stood up, with the wire-cutters in his hand. A second later, he was striding along by the side of the fence, looking for a spot that was dark, and out of sight of the road. Anne kept alongside him. Peter and Kate, as usual, lagged behind.

Suddenly they heard Barry saying: 'Ah. This spot should do.' He sounded so calm and confident that he might have been a professional burglar. There was something very professional, too, about the way he set to work on the fence. In about half a minute, there was a neat, circular hole in the mesh, about one metre in diameter – big enough for them all to crawl through with ease.

Although every time they'd heard the clip of the wire-cutters, Peter's and Kate's nerves had been as taut as the steel mesh itself, there had been no alarm bells, no blazing guns – no sounds at all, in fact, except the shrill whining of the wind through the wire, and the endless roaring of the traffic behind them on Rochester Road.

Anne and Peter had both brought lamps from their bicycles. Anne shone hers through the hole in the fence. It showed a long concrete path, stretching on and on, with the warehouses' rusty metal walls rearing up on either side. The rays of the torch didn't reach to the end of the path, so that it disappeared into total blackness, looking like a path to nowhere – or to the Unknown.

Kate shuddered. 'We've seen enough, haven't we? L-let's call it a night.'

'Not on your life!' said Anne. 'The fun's just starting. Come on, Barry – let's go!'

Barry clambered through the mesh first, with Anne just behind him.

Peter and Kate were slower. Very much slower. In fact, they were still standing, staring at the circular hole, when Anne and Barry had gone right down the path, and the light of Anne's bicycle lamp was just a flicker in the distance.

Then, suddenly, it disappeared, and there was nothing beyond the wire but blackness. Perhaps they had turned a corner and gone out of sight. Or perhaps . . . Peter didn't like to think of any more 'perhaps'es'.

'They're taking a terrible risk,' he said. Then he corrected himself. The Detectives had always done everything together, and this was no time to start changing that. 'I mean . . . *we're* taking a terrible risk,' he said, and somehow forced himself through the hole. He stood just the other side, waiting to help Kate through.

At that moment, from somewhere far away ahead of them, there came a yell, followed by an odd, echoing clang. That settled it. At the thought of Anne and Barry being in trouble, out in that sea of blackness, Peter's and Kate's nerves returned.

With a shout of 'The devil take all Devil Cats!' Kate was suddenly through the wire, and she and Peter were running down the path – straight into the weirdest experience in the Detectives' whole career.

6

'Good Evening, Intruders . . .'

It didn't take them long to catch up with Anne and Barry. They had turned into a side alley between two warehouses, about one hundred metres down the path on the right.

Anne was squatting on the ground, rubbing her head. Barry was standing over her.

'I tripped over an old tyre, lying in the path,' Anne said. 'And fetched my head up against that wall.' She pointed to the corrugated iron wall of a warehouse, just beside her. Peter flashed his torch on it, and shuddered. It was as rusty as the hulk of a salvaged ship, with nails standing out all over it.

'You must have given it quite a crack,' he said. 'We could hear the clang it made right back at the fence.'

Anne's aching head didn't improve her temper.

'You mean you still weren't through the hole by then? Talk about getting cold feet.'

'Cold our feet may be,' snorted Kate. 'But at least we look where we're going, and don't get them caught up in any old tyres that may be lying about. What in the world were you doing, anyway, going off the path before we'd caught up with you? This is no place for playing hide and seek.'

'It's no place for shouting, either,' Peter whispered tensely. Kate's shrill protests had sent tinny echoes rolling around the high metal walls that reared above them. 'You never know who or what we might find here, round any corner.'

'You're right there,' said Barry, in an equally tense whisper. 'We spotted something strange round this corner. That's why we turned down here. Look.'

He was holding Anne's bicycle lamp, and flashed its beam down the side alley, stretching out behind them. It was a narrow alley, barely one metre wide, running between the first and second of the five huge warehouses. Halfway down it they could see several large metal objects, more than a metre high and nearly one metre wide, totally blocking the path. Whatever they were, they were obviously brand new: the metal gleamed and sparkled, in startling contrast to the rusty iron of the warehouse walls on either side.

Peter whistled.

'Those must be the first of the machines,' he said. 'Probably brought in last night.'

'Yes. We'd got as far as figuring that out,' said Barry. 'But what sort of machines are they? I've never seen anything like them in my life. From here, they looked computerised – electronic – almost like something out of sci fi.'

Anne scrambled to her feet, still rubbing her head.

'Well, now that we're all together – at last,' she said pointedly, 'let's take a closer look.'

Taking her bicycle lamp from Barry, she started to lead the way down the side alley. The others followed in single file, Barry first, Peter next and Kate last. This time, nobody lagged behind. Peter was as keen as Barry to examine the mysterious equipment, and Kate had no desire to be left alone in this nightmare world of tinny echoes and dark alleys – where anything might lurk round any corner . . .

They had only taken about six paces when it happened.

From out of the darkness ahead of them or behind them – it sounded like both, but that might have been an echo effect – a deep, harsh voice boomed: '*Good evening, intruders.*'

Anne started so violently that she dropped her lamp. It fell with a clatter on to the concrete path, and went out – a tinkle of glass suggesting that it was out for good.

An almost total blackness closed in on them. The high walls lining the narrow alley cut out ninety per cent of the night sky. Peter was about to switch on his own bicycle lamp, but changed his mind. Perhaps someone was pointing a gun at them. Why let him know exactly where to fire?

Kate had turned on her heels, and was about to lead a quick retreat out of the alley, when the voice came again. This time it was deeper and harsher than ever, and so loud that it seemed to be booming and echoing deep inside their skulls.

'*Don't move,*' it said. '*Don't move an inch for ten seconds – or you will never intrude again.*'

'We'd better do what it says,' Anne whispered.

Nobody felt like arguing. The four remained absolutely motionless as the seconds passed. The whole time, Peter's sharp ears picked up faint clicking noises coming from the direction of those curious objects further down the alley.

At last, the seconds were up.

'*Thank you.*' said the voice politely. '*We have pictures of your faces now, even if you are masked. So do not think you are unknown to us, whoever you are. Now go – while you can.*'

The Detectives went – as fast as their legs could carry them.

They came bursting out of the side alley like bullets from a gun. Anne, Peter and Kate were all set to keep going, and not stop until they'd got clear through the hole in the mesh and away. Barry, though, seemed to have different ideas.

Half a dozen metres away from the side alley, he suddenly stopped dead. 'I just want to try something,' he murmured. 'Wait for me at the fence, folks. I'll catch you up.'

Then he calmly turned and strolled back into the alley.

'Come back!' Anne called after him. 'You're –you're being absolutely crazy – '

Barry didn't reply, but just kept walking.

Which left Anne no choice except to be absolutely crazy too. She wasn't going to allow a Detective to walk into serious danger by himself, even if it was his own stupid fault.

'Hang on,' she said. 'I'm coming too.'

Barry started. 'There's no need for that, honestly,' he said, over his shoulder. 'I wish you wouldn't . . .'

But he was too late. Anne was right behind him when he arrived at the spot where the voice had spoken to them before.

And the very second he reached it, the voice spoke again.

7

The Silent Shots

It used precisely the same words, too.

'*Good evening, intruders . . . Don't move. Don't move an inch for ten seconds, or you will never intrude again.*'

This time, Barry burst out laughing.

'And good evening to you, Friendly Neighbourhood Robot,' he drawled. Turning to Anne, he added: 'I had a feeling we'd been talking to nothing but a load of very advanced equipment. We'd better keep still for the ten seconds again, though, or it might fire off an atomising ray gun, or something. It's a good job I'm a great watcher of *Dr Who*.'

Just for a moment, Anne was too stunned to speak. Before she'd recovered herself, the ten seconds had elapsed and the taped voice had launched into the rest of its speech.

'*Thank you . . . We have pictures of your faces now, even if you are masked. So do not think you are unknown to us, whoever you are. Now go – while you can . . .*'

'If it's all the same to you, sunshine,' said Barry, 'we'd just as soon stay.'

Peter and Kate had caught up with them now. Both had heard everything that had happened – and, for the second time that night, were ashamed of their lack of nerve. Anxious to show that he didn't always have cold feet, Peter pushed past Anne and Barry, and walked right up to the strange machines, flashing his torch on the nearest of them.

Close to, the nearest machine looked a little like a TV camera, with its lens focused along the alley.

'Do you reckon it *could* have taken photos of us – even in the dark?' said Anne.

'And even through masks, if we'd been wearing them?' asked an awed Kate.

'It isn't impossible,' Peter said. 'I've read about infra-red cameras that can photograph faces in darkness, and through any sort of material, through the heat given off by a person's skin. This looks as if it might be one of them.'

'But it didn't just take our photos,' spluttered Kate. 'It said good evening to us, and threatened blue murder if we didn't keep still. What camera in the world could do things like that?'

Barry answered her. He was keen on electronics, and was saving up to buy his own computer.

'Any camera – with the right accessories, Katie me darling,' he said. 'This one's obviously got some kind of beam attachment. We broke the beam when we reached a certain point in the alley, and that triggered off the tape-recorded voice. And probably a blip on the tape triggered off the camera.'

Peter shuddered.

'I warned you all that the machines might be guarded. I never dreamed they'd be so way-out they could guard themselves!'

Anne decided it was time she got back to being leader. She walked up to Peter, and – without asking his permission – took charge of his bicycle lamp, now their only source of light.

'Well,' she began. 'Now that we know we've got the place to ourselves, I suggest we spend just a few more minutes exploring . . .'

Pushing past Peter, she flashed the lamp on to the other machines. 'Why,' she said. 'They're *all* like TV cameras . . .'

Peter's ears caught a very faint whirring noise.

'Come back!' he whispered urgently. 'You've started something.'

'What do you mean?' his sister snapped. Then she gasped. 'Hey! What do you think you're . . .'

Obeying some instinct he couldn't explain, Peter had seized her arm and yanked her backwards, right away from the machines.

Anne was taken completely by surprise. Strongarm stuff wasn't usually in Peter's line at all. She was so startled that she lost her balance, and fell heavily.

'Leggo!' she yelled, hoarse with fury. 'Have you completely flipped your – '

The bullets silenced her.

Three of them, one after the other, slammed into the concrete path at just the spot where she would have been standing if Peter hadn't yanked her backwards.

She knew that, because she happened to be shining the torch on the spot at the time, and its beam picked up three holes appearing from nowhere in the concrete, and thick white dust rising round them. There was no sound, apart from the *pthwack*! of the bullets' impact on the path. Whoever – whatever – was firing at them had a weapon that made no crack, no roar, not even the faintest *phutt*.

It was Barry who worked out where the shots were coming from. He'd glimpsed a flash high above them, a flaring pinprick of light stabbing out from the warehouse roof.

'Get down, everyone. There's a marksman up there with a rifle – oh, my God.' Barry's voice shot up three octaves, and became a high-pitched shriek. He'd suddenly realised that, from someone on the roof with night binoculars and a high-velocity rifle, they had no protection anywhere in the alley.

'Getting down's no good,' he screamed. 'There's only one answer. *Get moving*!'

'Now you're talking!' said Kate, her own voice, for once, too hoarse for screaming.

She was the first out of the side alley, but there wasn't much in it. The others were a split second behind her, and all four sprinted at Olympic speed back to the hole in the fence. If there was one marksman on the warehouse roofs, there could be others. There could be armed guards anywhere and everywhere, silent bullets flashing from any corner . . .

The Detectives were in a state of near-total panic, but that didn't stop first Anne, then Barry, then Peter getting through the hole in the mesh as fast as peas through a peashooter.

Kate didn't make it quite so fast. Halfway through, her mass of flaming red hair caught in the wire. Barry turned back, and cut her free by slicing through long strands of it with his penknife.

By this time, he'd recovered his nerve. In an almost perfect imitation of her Irish accent, he murmured: 'Tis a shocking shame, so it is, to be doing this to your crowning glory, Katie love.'

'Oh, shut up, will you, and just keep cutting!' Kate shrieked. She was shaking so violently that the whole stretch of fence started quivering.

'Take it easy,' said Peter. 'I think the danger's over.'

'What do you mean – over?' Kate yelled. 'Those men could be right behind us. We could get bullets in the back any – any second!'

'I don't think there are any men,' said Peter. 'I don't even think there was a marksman on the roof – just another automatic contraption, programmed to fire off bullets at that spot if anyone stepped too near the machines. I knew Anne had started some sinister machinery off. I heard the whirring. That's why I yanked her back . . .'

'And saved her life,' said Anne shakily. 'Th-thank you, Peter. I shan't forget it. And in future, I'll try not to rush into everything like a bull at a gate.'

Peter wasn't used to Anne being humble, and didn't like it.

'That'll be the day, dear sister,' he laughed awkwardly. 'That'll be the day.'

Kate was through the fence at last, and the Detectives went across the scrubland to pick up their bikes. They didn't lose any time getting on to them, and couldn't breathe easily until the warehouses were out of sight behind them. Not that they breathed too easily even then. It was just beginning to dawn on them what an extraordinary experience they'd had.

Kate was the first to start asking questions.

'I don't get any of this,' she said. 'We're supposed to be fighting a gang of criminals who are using those warehouses to hijack a lorry – perhaps a lorry carrying a load of bullion. Right?'

'That *was* right,' said Peter. 'But I think the theory wants changing now.'

'I was going to say,' said Kate. 'Why should criminals like that want to take photographs of people inspecting the equipment? Why should they say things like "Do not think you are unknown to us?" They don't sound like a gang of criminals to me. They sound more like . . .' Her eyes widened, and her bicycle started wobbling across the road as terrifying thoughts poured into her mind. '. . . more like creatures from outer space coming to take over England.'

'Steady, Katie, steady,' said Barry, as a car came charging past, missing Kate's right handlebar by centimetres. 'Rochester Road is no place to be dreaming up Daleks and little green men from flying saucers.'

'She's got a point, though,' said Anne. Her own eyes, for once, were almost as wide as Kate's. 'What sort of criminals use robot voices, and infra-red cameras, and silent rifles and – and –'

Peter continued for her.

'And equipment that must have cost hundreds of thousands of pounds,' he said softly. 'Really advanced equipment, too. Infra-red cameras are a very new thing – and I've never heard of *completely* silent rifles in my life! No kidding – we've seen stuff tonight that could have come straight out of a James Bond film.'

'A James Bond film!' yelped Kate.

With a great effort, she stopped her bike from wobbling all over the road again as she turned right round to face him.

'You mean – you think we're fighting *spies*?'

8

Alarm Call

The reply, from the careful, cautious Peter, stunned all three of the other Detectives.

'I don't see,' he said, 'that there's any other answer. Enemy agents are the only people I can imagine who would have equipment like that. It explains the photographic bit, too. They'd want to photograph intruders, to see if they were rival agents, British counter-spies or what. And they'd want to scare rival agents off by letting them know that they'd been photographed. "Do not think you are unknown to us" is a terrifying threat if there's the government of a powerful country behind it!'

'Ye-es,' said Barry thoughtfully. 'And just in case the other agents weren't scared off, and started nosing around their precious machines, they arranged for them to be shot on the spot. Instantly, automatically – and with bullets from a silent gun, so that there would be no noise to arouse the attention of even the sharpest-eared passer-by. You're right, Peter. We're up against an enemy spy network. We've got to be.'

His face, in the orange light from the lamp standards, was startled and awed. So, suddenly, was Anne's.

'Well, that's it, then, isn't it?' she said. 'Four twelve-year-olds can't take on an enemy like that.'

Barry was already beginning to recover his cool.

'Oh, I don't know,' he said. 'We've tackled drugs racketeers and murderers and even a Mafia mob. Don't let's lose our nerves.'

But Anne, for once, seemed to have lost hers completely.

'Don't talk rubbish,' she snapped. 'We're way out of our league and it's only common sense to admit it. We've got to bring Dad into this straight away.'

Peter was now sounding as awed as his sister.

'The CID won't be able to cope with this,' he said. 'They'll have to bring in Special Branch – or maybe MI6.'

For the rest of the way to their houses, the four cycled in silence, except for Barry's brief 'Good night' when he left them at the corner of his road. Peter, Anne and Kate were each trying to think of a good way to tell Detective Superintendent Miller that they'd cut a hole in a wire fence, thereby, in police language, 'breaking and entering' five warehouses. They wouldn't enjoy telling him about the bullets, either. Over and over again, he'd told them that they'd get themselves murdered one of these days. They couldn't deny that tonight, one of them very nearly had . . .

As it happened, Mr Miller was out late on a case that evening, so they decided to postpone talking to him until tomorrow.

'*First* thing tomorrow,' Anne promised herself as she climbed into bed.

She set her alarm clock for a quarter to seven, intending to be first down in the morning, and to take her father and mother tea in bed. That usually put her father in a good mood for the day.

It wasn't the alarm bell, though, that woke Anne up next morning. It was the deafening clanging of the telephone downstairs in the hall. She looked at her watch, and saw that it was 6.33 and 11 seconds. Oh, well, she thought. Perhaps she could put her father in a good mood by going down to answer the phone. If it was a wrong number, she'd have saved him getting out of bed. Though she'd have to call him, of course, if it was a police emergency.

She didn't bother to put on a dressing gown or slippers, but went haring downstairs barefoot in her bright red pyjamas. Being Anne, she moved so fast that she was picking up the receiver before the bell had finished its second ring.

It wasn't a wrong number – and it *was* an emergency, though not a police one.

The caller was Barry, sounding very tense. 'Sorry to wake you up – but have you spoken to your father yet?'

'No. He came in late last night, after we went to bed. I was going to take him up a cup of tea at around seven, and tell him then.'

'Well – don't. At least until we've talked it over.'

Anne didn't like being given orders by anyone. 'And just why shouldn't I?' she snapped.

'I'll tell you,' said Barry. 'I've just had a phone call from Phil. He sounded in a shocking state – scared half out of his wits.'

'Sure it wasn't just his flu?'

'No. He never had any flu at all, he told me. Peter's guess was right. His father *did* catch him stealing those keys. There was a terrible row, which ended with Phil being locked in his room until he'd told the old boy everything he knew.'

'Tough,' said Anne. 'But why should that stop me talking to Dad?'

Barry's voice suddenly became very dramatic.

'Mr Pearson had a visitor an hour ago – just before dawn. A man with a hat pulled over his eyes so that no one could see his face. Phil was dragged out of bed and had to go downstairs and meet him. "Admit it!" the man said. "You have been talking to your schoolmates – the Dean Street Detectives. They were at the warehouses last night. We know that because we took their photographs, and have compared them with the newspaper cuttings on our files." '

Anne was sounding pretty tense herself now.

'I suppose that these spies, or whatever they are, moved the rest of their machines into the warehouses in the middle of the night – and, at the same time, checked their camera to see if there'd been any intruders,' she mused. 'It must be a kind of instant camera to give results so fast. Well, go on. What did the visitor do next?'

'Apparently, he seized hold of Phil and started shaking him.'

'While his father just watched?'

'Mr Pearson is a frightened man – with a weak heart. He just stood there, shivering, as far as I can make out, while the visitor told Phil: "Ring up the Dean Street Detectives as soon as it is light – and give them this message. If they make a single move against us, or whisper one word of this to Detective Superintendent Miller, we shall have no mercy on your father or mother – or you!" '

Anne's voice became cold and angry.

'I see. Very clever of them,' she said softly. 'They don't threaten us directly. They know that wouldn't do much good. But they threaten us through this helpless, hopeless family – the father with a weak heart and his fat, stupid son . . .'

'Wait a minute,' said Barry. 'Fat boys aren't necessarily stupid, you know. And Phil was bright enough to come to *us* for help!'

'Help which we can't possibly give him now,' said Anne, 'without putting all the Pearsons in danger.'

'We might work out a way,' said Barry. 'But it'll be out of our hands once you talk to Mr Miller.'

Anne frowned. Barry was a born outlaw type, who

hated bringing the police into anything if it could possibly be helped. Usually she agreed with him, but this case was different. They were up against enemy agents, and had no idea what was really going on. For all they knew, all Britain might be in danger –

'I can't help that,' she said at length, her eyes gleaming. 'It still seems that the only sensible thing to do is to bring Dad into this straight away. The CID will give the Pearsons protection – or if they don't, Special Branch or MI6 will.'

'I hope you're right,' said Barry. 'We're up against some very ruthless people, remember.'

'I know that,' said Anne. 'That's precisely why I don't think we should keep this to ourselves any . . .'

She broke off. Mrs Miller had been woken up by the bell, and was coming down the stairs behind her.

'Er – good morning, Mum,' she said, mainly to let Barry know that she had company.

'Good morning, dear. You're up bright and early.'

Mrs Miller didn't ask Anne who was calling her at such an unearthly hour. She was used to the Detectives doing crazy things at crazy times, and was past being alarmed – or even surprised – by most of them. One thing, though, did seem to worry her.

'Did I hear you say you were planning to wake Dad up to tell him something? Well, please don't. He didn't get to bed till nearly five, and desperately needs some sleep. Can't it possibly wait until you get back from school this evening?'

Very reluctantly, Anne said that she supposed it *could* wait until then.

Until then, she told herself, but not a moment longer.

No matter what Barry said, no matter what the risk to the Pearsons, she couldn't let the Detectives stay silent – on the night that the Devil Cat was passing . . .

9

Eavesdropper

That day turned out to be the most frightening one that the Detectives had ever spent at Dean Street School.

It began with the news that Phil Pearson wasn't coming into school. His father had apparently telephoned the school with the old story that his son had flu.

'I suppose that means he's locked him in his room again,' said Kate. 'If I were Phil I'd have a few words with my father – even if he does have a weak heart. The man seems so scared of these spies it isn't true!'

'To be honest,' said Peter, shuddering, 'I'm pretty scared of them myself. People who rig up machines that fire bullets can't really be too nice to know. They'd be callous enough to carry out all their threats without thinking twice about it.'

Anne turned her head angrily.

'You sound as if you agreed with Barry. He thinks that we should just sit tight, and not do or say anything at all, in case his precious Pearson gets hurt. Isn't that right, Barry?'

It was the lunch break, and the Detectives were in their consulting room, having an urgent secret conference. They had brought sandwiches with them but, so far, they'd remained untouched. For once, the four were too jumpy even to eat.

Not that Barry looked jumpy. He was in his favourite spot, lounging against the wall by the Humphrey Bogart poster, and apparently as cool as though they were discussing football scores. But a bright red spot on each cheek, and a dangerous glint in his eyes showed that beneath the surface he wasn't at ease at all.

'That was *not* right,' he snapped. 'I didn't say anything about us sitting tight and doing nothing. As all of you ought to know by now, I'm much more in favour of standing up and doing plenty. But a fat chance we'll have of that if we call in Detective Superintendent Miller! We'll probably find ourselves locked in a room, with a CID man guarding the door.'

'Let's stop fighting and take a vote on it,' said Kate. 'That's the proper democratic thing to do.'

'A very good idea!' said Anne enthusiastically. 'Keep quiet, then, everybody. I'll explain exactly what I think, and then hands up everyone who agrees.'

'*That's* not democratic!' yelled Kate. 'What about what I think – and Peter thinks – and Barry thinks – and –'

At that moment, something very odd happened. Kate was perching, as usual, on the arm of Peter's chair. Peter, for once, wasn't leaning back with his eyes narrowed. He was hunched up, nervous and tense, scribbling furiously on the back of an envelope. Kate looked over his shoulder, saw what he was writing – and immediately started talking like a cracked record.

'– and Peter thinks – and *I* think – and Barry thinks – and Peter thinks – and –'

While Anne and Barry stared in astonishment, Kate snatched the envelope and held it up so that they could both see what Peter had written.

THERE'S SOMEONE LISTENING OUTSIDE THE DOOR. BUT KEEP TALKING. DON'T LET HIM KNOW WE KNOW!

Kate desperately tried to keep talking, getting into more and more of a muddle all the time.

'I mean, until we know what everybody votes – er, vote what everybody thinks – er . . .'

'Oh, do pull yourself together, Kate,' said Anne sharply. 'Anybody would think you were going round the twist.' Struggling to keep her own voice normal, she went on: 'But all right, I'll do as you say. We'll hear what everyone has to say in turn – starting with you, Peter.'

She chose Peter, because Barry was already tiptoeing across the room to the door.

It wasn't a very good choice. Peter started violently, and was complete tongue-tied for at least two seconds – during which Barry stepped on a loose floorboard, which gave an ominous creak.

Peter, Anne and Kate started talking all at once.

'Come on, Peter,' said Anne. 'I asked you what you thought.'

'I – er – I – er – well, that is, I think –' spluttered Peter.

'Vote – think – vote – think – vote,' said Kate, just for the sake of adding to the noise.

What it all sounded like outside the door, none of them could imagine. But suddenly it didn't matter. With one bound – which somehow he made to look like a casual stroll – Barry was by the door. A split-second later, he had hurled it open.

The eavesdropper was so startled that he lost his balance, and fell forward into the room. But he picked himself up rapidly and stood, blinking round with large, watery eyes.

'So this is where the famous Detectives meet, yes?' said Mr Gorodny.

The Detectives were almost as taken aback as Gorodny had been. It was the first time that anyone on the Dean Street School staff had found out about the consulting room. Heaven knew how many school rules they were breaking in using it . . .

Anne found her voice at last.

'Er – yes, this *is* where we meet,' she said awkwardly. 'We know it's out of bounds, but didn't think we were doing much harm in taking it over. It hasn't been used by the school for anything for years and years.'

Mr Gorodny frowned.

'Nevertheless, it *is* – how do you say – out of bounds, and by rights, I should report you to the Head Teacher, yes?'

The Detectives said nothing, for the simple reason that they had nothing to say.

Mr Gorodny looked for a moment as though he was going to start weeping. But the opposite happened. Those watery eyes crinkled at the corners and he was suddenly all smiles.

'But this I have decided not to do,' he announced. 'After all, you are famous people. You have brought honour to the school. That deserves special treatment – so not to worry, please. Your secret is safe with me.' He looked at his watch, and gave them a final, mischevious smile. 'That is – if you are punctual for my next lesson. In five minutes it will be two o'clock, when I teach French to 4G. If you are not there, Peter, Anne and Kate, I come down here to fetch you. With the Head!'

Chuckling, he gave them all a bow, and turned to the door. Barry held it open for him, and a moment later, he had scuttled away down the corridor.

As soon as he'd gone, Kate said, shuddering: 'Ugh. That *horrible* man. He's evil – I've always felt it.'

'Be fair,' said Anne. 'It was pretty nice of him to promise not to give us away.'

Peter's eyes narrowed. 'Yes,' he murmured. 'He's pretty nice – as far as lousy, stinking foreign agents go.'

The others started.

'You really think he's a spy?' said Anne.

'He was spying on *us*, wasn't he?' Peter said. 'And it's a bit of a coincidence that he should start doing that the day after we get our photographs taken by the enemy network. And only a few hours after the Pearsons get all those threats.'

He suddenly shot out of his armchair, and started burrowing in the linen chest where he kept his magnifying glasses and powders. Producing a tin of powder, he walked out into the corridor, and started shaking it over all the floorboards, between the consulting room door and the staircase.

'No one can walk on this stuff without leaving very clear foot-prints,' he said over his shoulder. 'So we'll know if anyone comes down here nosing about after we've gone.'

'What's the good of taking footprints if you can't tell who they belong to?' said Kate. 'You wouldn't even recognise Mr Gorodny's if you saw them.'

'Oh, yes, I would,' said Peter. 'Hadn't you noticed? Gorodny's got very small feet for a man. Must take only size five shoes. He walks in a funny way, too, with his toes turned in.'

Barry was smiling sardonically as he watched all this.

'Talk about locking the stable door after the horse has bolted!' he murmured. 'In case you hadn't noticed, Mr Gorodny's been and gone. He won't be back – unless you three are late for his lesson, which is very likely, seeing that it's one minute to two!'

The Detectives locked up their consulting room, and hurried off along the corridor. Their footprints showed up as clearly on Peter's powder as though they were making tracks through snow.

The sight of them gave Kate a strange feeling. They made her think of the Abominable Snowman . . . and suddenly, from out of nowhere, came a hunch that something abominable was going to happen. Soon. To *her* . . .

Before she could tell the others about the feeling – or even describe it clearly to herself – the two o'clock school bell sounded from upstairs. She started running to catch up with Peter and Anne, and soon they were off to 4G, to be taught by a man who was either a kindly nincompoop . . . or one of the deadliest enemies they had ever known.

10

The Vanishing Detective

Nothing much happened during Mr Gorodny's second lesson with 4G. He came near to weeping several times, but that was apparently caused by the class's absolute hopelessness at French, not by any uproar.

The Detectives were no brighter than anyone else, partly because their minds were on other things; things that became more frightening as the seconds ticked by, bringing them closer and closer to the night when the Devil Cat would be passing. Peter was asking himself for the hundredth thousandth time what that term could mean. Obviously 'Devil Cat' was a code-name for something – probably something that travelled by road. But what could it possibly be? Kate was still struggling to forget that terrible feeling that had come over her in the corridor downstairs: the Corridor of Ghosts again – how she hated that place! Anne was remembering, with a start, that they still hadn't settled the question of whether or not she should talk to Dad. This wasn't something they could very well discuss when bicycling home through all the traffic, and once they got home, her father himself would be around, and might overhear anything they said. They'd have to hold another conference down in the consulting room before they left, she decided. Being Anne, she also decided that somehow, she'd *make* them see things her way . . . and less than five minutes after the conference started, she had done precisely that.

'Whatever the Devil Cat is, it's something foreign agents are after – foreign agents with years-ahead equipment!' She spoke briskly, in her ringing 'Headmistress' voice. 'The four of us can't hope to stop them getting it on our own. And if we don't tell the authorities, and the Devil Cat is seized, we could have put the whole of Britain – maybe the whole of the world – in danger! Are any of you going to argue with *that*?'

'I'm not, for one, dear sister,' Peter grinned. 'I never ate those sandwiches at lunchtime, and I'd like to get home to tea.'

'I'm not arguing, either,' said Kate. Her terrifying feeling was getting stronger and stronger, and she wanted to get home too.

The three of them looked at Barry, who managed a faint, wry smile. 'I was never any good at arithmetic, but even I can see that it's three to one against me,' he said, adding very quietly: 'I only hope that doesn't mean that it's three to one against Phil and his parents staying alive.'

There was an awkward silence, during which the Detectives felt cold, scared and uncertain about what was the right thing to do. Except Anne, who was never uncertain about any decision once she'd made it.

'Right, then,' she said briskly. 'That's settled. Meeting adjourned. Let's go.'

Like Peter, she was suddenly hungry, and eager for home and tea. She shot out of the room and raced along the corridor to the back staircase, which led up to the main part of the school. Barry was alongside her, and Peter only just behind.

Kate, on the other hand, was a long way behind.

The moment she stepped out of the consulting room on to the footprint-powdered floorboards of that dreaded corridor, a kind of panic seized her.

She had had many strange, uncanny hunches in her life, having inherited second sight from her father, Detective Sergeant Murphy. He had been nicknamed 'Spooky' because of his ability to sense where criminals were hiding or where corpses were buried. But Kate had never had a feeling as terrifying as this. A voice seemed to be thundering through her brain telling her: '*You're in danger. Terrible danger. It's here. It's creeping up on you. Run. Run for your life . . .*'

But, exactly as in a nightmare, she was so terrified she couldn't move. Desperately, she struggled to reason with her feelings.

'Now just you pull yourself together, Katie Murphy,' she told herself severely – aloud, so that it would drown that other voice in her brain. 'There's nothing to be afraid of. You've walked down this stupid, spooky corridor hundreds of times before. What in the world are you carrying on like this for? Do you want the others to say you've gone craz – oh, Holy Mother of –'

Her voice rose to a shriek as she heard a soft footstep right behind her.

By this time, Anne, Peter and Barry were up the back staircase, and had slipped out into one of the main corridors of the school. It was a long, dark corridor, crowded with children hurrying for the cloakrooms to collect coats and caps before starting for home. There was such a din all round that even Peter's sharp ears couldn't pick up Kate's scream, echoing round the basement far below.

The three, in fact, had gone some way down the corridor, carried along by the throng, when Barry suddenly pointed out that they *were* only three.

Anne's mind was still focused on the coming talk with her father, and she hardly heard him.

'Kate? Oh, she must be just behind us somewhere,' she said, without bothering to look back.

Peter and Barry did look back, but weren't too worried when they still failed to spot Kate's red hair amongst the bobbing heads behind them.

Dean Street School was a maze of corridors. Kate could have turned off into another one, as a short cut to the cloakroom, or met a friend and stopped to chat. They'd see her at the shed in a couple of minutes, when they'd got their coats, and had gone out to collect their bikes ...

There was a big crowd at the cycle shed, and it took them another half-minute to realise that Kate simply wasn't there. And that they'd seen no sign of her since they'd all rushed out of the consulting room about five minutes before.

They were worried then, all right. Without a word, they turned on their heels, and didn't stop running until they were back on the basement staircase leading down to the Corridor of Ghosts.

Peter stretched out a hand, and stopped the others when they were on the bottom steps. From where they were standing, they had a good view of the bare floor of the corridor, now white with the powder he'd sprinkled all over it. Dozens of footprints showed on this powdered surface, all the way from the door of the consulting room in the distance to the foot of the stairs.

'Not that we can learn a lot from those,' said Peter. 'Since I sprinkled the powder, we've been along the corridor three times: once going *to* the consulting room and twice coming back.'

'There are your *going* footprints – see, Barry?' said

Anne. 'And there are the ones you made coming back. And those are mine – and those are Peter's – and those rather smaller ones are Kate's. She's always had tiny feet.'

'Er. Yes. I see,' said Barry. He was beginning to feel a little lost. Anne and Peter – and Kate, for that matter – had been experimenting with footprints and fingerprints since they were five years old. But he'd never been part of Miller-Murphy Investigations, and could hardly tell one footprint from another. 'Can't we move on now?' he said.

'Just one more second,' said Peter. He was leaning forward now, very tensely, peering hard at the traces at their feet. 'There is something very strange here. Have you noticed it, Anne?'

Anne was nodding.

'I've noticed it all right. We three have left twice as many coming-back tracks as Kate. Which means –'

'Which means,' said Peter softly, 'that the last time we came back along the corridor, Kate wasn't with us at all. It's – it's almost as though she never left the consulting room.'

'But that's crazy!' said Barry. 'Why should she have stayed there when the rest of us were . . .'

He broke off. Neither Peter nor Anne were listening to him. Both were hurrying down the corridor, peering at the tracks as they went. All he could do was dazedly stand and watch, feeling a very useless member of the team. 'Shouldn't you look in the consulting room?' he asked suddenly. 'She may be in there now – having a fainting fit or something!'

Anne and Peter were by the consulting room door. Anne threw it open and glanced inside the room.

'Nobody here,' she reported.

Barry stared. 'Sorry if I'm being stupid,' he said,

'but surely, if she didn't come out into the corridor, she *must* be there. Unless she vanishes in a puff of good old Irish smoke.'

He tried to sound cool, but stumbled over his words. He was now desperately worried about Kate. So were Anne and Peter, although they calmly kept on with their Miller-Murphy-style investigations.

Peter was once again being a complete Sherlock Holmes. He dived into the consulting room, and came out with a magnifying glass. Then he went down on his knees to peer at some peculiar tracks immediately outside the consulting room door. Suddenly his face turned almost as white as the powder.

'I think I've got the answer,' he said grimly. 'Come and look.'

As Anne and Barry stood over him, he pointed to what looked like very small footprints, very badly smudged.

'See these? I think they were made by Kate. They're side by side, which means that she wasn't walking or running when she made them, but standing still –here in the corridor, just outside the door. It looks as though she set out to follow us, but stopped dead . . . probably felt faint or had the heebie-jeebies, or something.'

'But she couldn't have stood there for ever,' said Barry. 'Aren't there any signs of her walking in any direction afterwards?'

Peter's voice became grimmer.

'Not of her *walking* anywhere, no,' he said. 'The prints are smudged – and – see? – they turn into two long troughs in the powder. It looks as though someone came up behind her and dragged her backwards. There are no scuffle marks, so she didn't struggle. Probably he . . .' His words were stumbling like Barry's now. 'Probably he knocked her out.'

‘Someone came up behind her?’ said Barry huskily. ‘But – who?’

‘Don’t be so silly,’ snapped Anne. ‘How can you possibly expect Peter to know that?’

She had underestimated her brother.

‘As a matter of fact, I think I *do* know,’ Peter said. ‘There are two footprints here that don’t belong to Kate, or Anne, or you or me. Just the two . . . suggesting that the man who made them came creeping up on Kate from the other end of the corridor, where I hadn’t spread the powder. Fortunately, though, he stepped in it once, just here outside the consulting room door. So I can tell you that he wears size five shoes . . . with toes turned inwards. In other words, Kate’s attacker was . . .’

In voices hoarse, not with fear now, but with hate and fury, Anne and Barry finished the sentence for him.

‘*Gorodny*!’

11

Explosive Warning

Peter hadn't finished, even then. Like a bloodhound picking up a scent, he suddenly shot off down the corridor, in the opposite direction from the staircase. There was no sprinkled powder on that stretch of the corridor, but that didn't matter. Gorodny having stepped on the powder, his soles and heels still bore traces of it, and his footprints continued to show up clearly.

They led Peter – and Anne and Barry, who were just behind him – out of the corridor, down a passage, up a flight of stone steps and through a door out into a weed-strewn part of what had once been the school's back garden. A concrete path ran from the door down to a gate at the end of this garden. The footprints could still be spotted going along the path.

'What's happened to Kate's footprints?' asked Anne.

'There's no sign of them,' said Peter. 'And there would have been if she'd walked anywhere – because, remember, she'd stepped on that powder too. Which can only mean one thing. After Gorodny dragged her backwards, he knocked her out – and then picked her up and carried her. Yes, look!' At one point, Gorodny had stepped off the path for a moment and left a footprint in a flowerbed. 'See how deep that print goes? Nearly four centimetres into the earth! Gorodny's a small man – doesn't weigh enough to make a deep print like that on his own. So that *proves* he was carrying Kate.'

'How can you be sure that she was unconscious?' asked Barry.

'If she wasn't, she'd have been kicking and screaming,' said Peter. 'And no one could carry a kicking and screaming Kate without his footsteps wobbling all over the place! No. Kate was unconscious all right. Or –'

He couldn't bring himself to say any more.

Anne shivered. 'Can't – can't we go faster?'

Peter was already moving as fast as he could. But the powder had been wearing off Gorodny's shoes by the time he reached this spot; the prints were getting fainter. Very soon, it might not be possible to make them out at all.

They had reached the gate at the end of the garden now. Peter opened it, and a second later, he, Anne and Barry found themselves on the pavement of a narrow lane at the back of the school building, used by one or two of the teachers for parking their cars.

Gorodny had evidently stepped in a puddle. His wet footprints showed up clearly crossing the pavement – but they stopped dead at the kerb, and did not appear again.

'What's happened?' said Anne stupidly. 'He couldn't have vanished into thin air!'

'No, dummy. But he could have bundled Kate into the back of his car, climbed in after her, and driven away!' said Peter. 'And it's pretty obvious that that's just what he did.'

Anne was suddenly close to tears – tears of rage, with herself and the others.

'In other words – we've let poor Kate be kidnapped right under our noses, and the kidnapper's got clean away!' she choked. 'How *could* we have been so dim?

We knew Gorodny was fond of sneaking about in the corridor. That's why you put down the powder! If only we'd taken a bit more care. It's my fault – I'm the leader . . .'

'Stop that!' said Barry sharply. 'There's no point going around blaming ourselves. We couldn't possibly have known that Gorodny was planning anything like this. To tell you the truth, I still can't make out why he's done it.'

'I can,' said Peter. 'Look at it this way. The one thing the spy network fears is that the police – or MI6 – should get to the warehouse and seize their machines before tonight, when the Devil Cat passes. That's why they sent that man round to the Pearson's house at dawn this morning – to make sure that Phil and his father and mother kept quiet, *and through Phil, to terrify us into keeping quiet too*! But it didn't work, did it? We were getting set to tell Dad all about the warehouse this evening, as soon as we got home. We were taking a vote on that very thing when Gorodny was eavesdropping on us at lunchtime.'

Barry whistled. 'So we were! You reckon, then, that Gorodny got desperate and, at the first opportunity, kidnapped Kate to keep our mouths shut?'

'But that doesn't make sense,' said Anne. 'Surely we're liable to do more talking now than ever!' Her eyes were dry, but gleaming with fury. 'I'm not even going to wait until we get home. I'm going to a call box, to ring Dad straight away . . .'

'I think you'd better wait,' said Peter quietly, 'until we've examined – this.'

He had spotted a large brown envelope lying on the pavement just in front of the gate. He had been concentrating so hard on the footprints that he had missed it before. He picked it up, and held it out so that the others could see the words scrawled on the front of it.

TO THE DEAN STREET DETECTIVES.
URGENT!
OPEN IMMEDIATELY, PLEASE!

Peter obediently opened it – and took out a small cassette player.

'He's no fool, Gorodny, is he?' said Barry. 'He must have realised that he was leaving footprints – and that we'd follow him as far as here.'

'But this is crazy,' said Anne. 'If Peter's right and he was carrying Kate in his arms or over his shoulder, how could he stop and record messages for us?'

'He must have done it sitting in the car,' said Peter, 'after he'd put Kate in the back seat – or more probably, on the floor at the back, hidden under a mack or something. Then, obviously, he chucked the envelope out of the window before he drove away, and it slithered across the pavement to the gate.'

Anne was still shivering – or, perhaps, quivering with anger.

'But how *could* he sit there behind the wheel talking into a cassette-recorder, with poor Kate lying there unconscious behind him? Supposing someone had come by, someone who knew him?'

Peter shrugged. 'Secret agents are paid to take risks. And that wasn't a big one. This is a very quiet road. Come on. We'd better go back to the consulting room and play this. We can listen to it properly there.'

He started to lead the way again, but was walking too slowly for Anne. She snatched the cassette out of his hands, charged through the garden gate and ran all the way back to the consulting room, with a breathless Barry and a panting Peter behind her.

She banged the cassette player down on top of the linen chest, and pressed the ON switch.

Almost immediately, they heard the familiar voice of Mr Gorodny. Unbelievably, he seemed to be trying to sound friendly.

'This is a message for the Dean Street Detectives,' he began. 'I have very good news for you. There is no need to worry about your brave, sweet little Kate. We have had to take her away from you, but she is absolutely unharmed –'

'Oh, yes?' said Barry roughly. 'You've only bashed her on the head and have her lying there unconscious, you . . .'

'Quiet!' hissed Anne and Peter, the Miller twins for once talking as one.

Barry struggled to keep his temper, but it became harder and harder as the voice went on.

'I am happy to tell you that Kate will be back with you safe and sound first thing tomorrow. *If* . . . ah, yes, I am afraid there is just a little *if* . . .'

'He means – here comes the big threat,' whispered Peter. And he was right. Gorodny's voice suddenly changed completely and became harsh and menacing.

'You must say absolutely nothing to Detective Superintendent Miller about me – or about the Pearsons – or about what you saw at the warehouse. We shall know immediately if you do, because Miller will obviously send CID men to the warehouses to investigate. If that should happen, Kate will die – instantly.'

There was a pause. Then suddenly Mr Gorodny was trying to be friendly again.

'Believe me, I do not like threatening children in this way, but I have no choice, you understand, no choice at all. And your ordeal – it will not be very long. Tomorrow morning, Kate will be free, I and my colleagues will be gone, the Pearson family will have no more to worry about, everybody's nightmare will be over. That's if you don't talk. But if you do . . .'

Gorodny's voice was suddenly drowned by a loud fizzing. Barry started fiddling with the tuning knob.

'No, don't adjust it!' yelled Peter. 'Turn it off!'

Startled, Barry obeyed. But the fizzing didn't stop. It became louder, almost deafening.

'Get back – down!' yelled Peter.

The Detectives hurriedly drew back, ducking – just in time. The cassette player suddenly exploded like a firework – a very dangerous firework. Bits of metal pinged against the walls all round the room. Suddenly the whole instrument was blazing furiously with a heat that reduced it in seconds to a puddle of smouldering molten plastic. The top of the linen chest was scorched and blackened. Thick smoke, smelling like a bonfire of old tyres, filled the room, and sent them out into the corridor, coughing and choking and with their eyes streaming.

'Strewth,' gasped Peter. 'A self-destruct set. They're up to all the tricks, aren't they?'

It was more than the smoke that was choking Anne. It was a feeling of helpless fury.

'They've got us, those ruddy ratbags. We'll have to do as they say. We just can't bring in Dad now.'

Barry mopped his streaming eyes, and suddenly smiled. It was a tough, cold smile, exactly like Bogart's on the poster back in the consulting room.

Like Bogart, he didn't waste words. In fact, he only used one – but it caused almost as big an explosion as the cassette-player.

'Good,' he said.

12

No Go

Anne was the first to round on him.

'What do you mean – good?'

'What I say,' Barry drawled. 'This whole thing suits me fine. I always did believe that we'd do better to tackle these spies on our own. That's what we've done with all the other villains we've fought, after all. Why should they be so different?'

'I'll tell you,' said Peter. 'It's because they're immensely clever, tremendously well-equipped agents, with a vast international organisation behind them. And what they're carrying out is a cunning operation, planned down to the smallest detail, probably months in advance. For example, why do you suppose they planted Gorodny here? Because they knew they were going to put the squeeze on the Pearson family, and this is the school that Mr Pearson's son attends. They must have found out somehow that Phil was friendly with you – one of the Dean Street Detectives. They realised that Phil might discover something, and pass it on to us. Even if they ordered Mr Pearson to keep him away from school, we might get suspicious and start nosing about – and tell our father, who'd start the CID nosing about, too. So Gorodny arrived to keep a close watch on both Phil and us.'

'I get it!' said Anne. 'That's why he sailed in to

rescue Barry and Phil from the skinheads. It was to try and make friends with them.'

'That's right,' said Peter. 'And, of course, that's why he's shown such an intense interest in us from the start. As for that weeping business, well, maybe it was an act, and maybe it wasn't. Even secret agents are human – and it can't have been easy for someone with no teacher training to get up and face class after class of Dean Street roughs. If he had some kind of nervous trouble affecting his eyes, that was just the sort of thing to bring it out.'

'You really think he's not a teacher at all?' said Barry. 'Then how on earth did he get the Head to take him on?'

'Forged testimonials from some swanky school, I suppose,' Peter said. 'As I keep saying, these people are up to all the tricks. Or he could have proper teaching qualifications. It would be a good cover, in spite of his habit of weeping.' His eyes narrowed. 'And tonight they're going to be up to the biggest trick of all. I only wish to Heaven we could get some clue about what it is. Not that there's much we could do about it, I suppose, even if we did know.'

He expected Anne to disagree, but she nodded her head.

'We've got to face it,' she said. 'As things stand, we'd be crazy to do *anything*. If we breathe a word about this to anyone, it'd be like putting Kate's head in a noose. And the worst of it is, we'd be risking her life just as much if we made any move at all! I hate to say it, but Gorodny could be right. It may be best just to wait until the nightmare's over, and Kate comes back safe and sound tomorrow morning.'

There was a long, awkward pause. Then: '*If* she comes back safe and sound,' said Barry softly. 'We've only got Gorodny's word that she will. And if you think we can trust him, I'm afraid I don't.' Suddenly it was his turn to round on Anne. 'What's come over you, O fearless leader? Ever since you nearly got hit by those bullets last night, you've been all jittery about this case. It isn't like you at all.'

Anne turned crimson.

'The bullets had nothing to do with it!' she shouted. Then her voice softened. 'But maybe the sight of those space-age machines did. And the thought of the vast, million-pound outfit behind them. I said at the time: "This is too big for us to handle" and everything that's happened since has proved me right.'

Barry stared at her coldly.

'But you've always been an "action-at-all-costs" girl. That's what I admire about you.'

'There wouldn't be much to admire,' said Anne steadily, 'if I okayed action – at the cost of Kate's life.'

Her face was still red, and her eyes were glittering. It was costing her a lot to fight her own nature, and insist that they did nothing. But she was still certain that that was the only possible course.

'We don't know enough to act yet, anyhow,' she went on. 'We've no idea where they've taken Kate. We haven't a clue why they've put those machines in those warehouses – or what they are there to do. We do know that they're complicated and dangerous – and that they've brought in more of them since last night. If we go blundering down there, we're bound to get spotted – by some super infra-red spy camera or whatever – and all we'll have done is give them a good reason for murdering Kate.'

'If you feel that way,' said Barry coldly, 'maybe I'll nip down there on my own.'

Whether or not she was ordering action, Anne could

still be commanding. 'Oh, no, you won't,' she said.

'And why not?'

'Because I'm the leader – and I say no.'

For a moment, it looked as though Barry was going to rebel. But then he remembered that everything the Detectives had achieved, they had achieved together. And they had achieved it under Anne. So he just shrugged, and said, rather bitterly: 'Okay, okay. We do nothing and say nothing, act dumb and stay dumb, until we hear those long-forgotten words: "Let's go".'

'That's right,' said Anne. 'And I'll promise you one thing. I won't forget them for one minute longer than I can help.'

She led the way back to the consulting room, to make sure the exploding cassette player hadn't started a fire. The smoke had cleared from the room, and all that could be seen of what had happened was the charred top of the linen chest, and a little puddle of molten plastic, rapidly becoming cold and hard.

'They're certainly thorough,' said Peter, awed at the sight. 'There's not a scrap of evidence now that Gorodny threatened us at all. People would even have to take our word for it that that had once been a cassette player.'

Shuddering, the Detectives hurried off to the cycle shed. They didn't exactly enjoy collecting their bikes. The sight of Kate's machine, left all by itself in the rack, brought lumps to their throats.

If they made one wrong move, Anne reminded herself grimly, Kate would never be around to ride that bike again. No matter what, she *had* to insist that they kept their mouths shut and didn't do anything rash at all.

Keeping their mouths shut wasn't the main problem when the three arrived at the Millers' home. It was having to open them, and tell some plausible lie to account for Kate not being with them.

'She – she got a last-minute invite to a birthday party,' said Anne.

'That's right. At Belinda Brown's,' added Peter, inventing the name on the spur of the moment.

Mrs Miller blinked. 'Belinda who?'

'Brown,' said Peter, more firmly than ever. 'You must have met her, Mum. Tall girl. Fair hair. Thick spectacles. Squints.'

'She gives pretty weird parties,' Anne added. 'So don't expect Kate back till late. In fact, she might be asked to stay the night.'

Mrs Miller frowned. She was used to the children doing all kinds of things, but not to one of them staying out all night without the slightest warning. 'I'd better ring the Browns up about this,' she said. 'Where do they live?'

'No idea, I'm afraid,' said Peter, thankful that he'd picked a common name. There were pages of Browns in the phone book – far too many for his mother to ring round them all.

'Not to worry, though,' said Anne, as breezily as she could. 'The Browns are a very nice family. Belinda's father's a . . .' She picked the safest-sounding profession she could think of: '. . . a solicitor, I think.'

'Huh!' said Mrs Miller. 'I'll have the law on *him* if he doesn't bring Kate back till tomorrow morning! All-night parties at *her* age! I've never heard of such a thing! Why, she doesn't have anything with her – pyjamas, or dressing-gown, or even a toothbrush!' Suddenly she was staring hard at Anne. 'What's the matter? You look as though you're going to start crying!'

'She's just jealous,' said Peter, swiftly. 'She was

hoping Belinda Brown would invite her too.'

'By the way,' said Anne, desperately trying to change the subject, 'since you'll have cooked for the three of us, we thought we'd ask Barry round to tea. I hope you don't mind.' She was anxious for the Detectives to stay together – the ones that were left.

Mrs Miller didn't mind. Barry was always welcome, she said. And suddenly she remembered something that took her mind off Kate. 'Oh, and you'll be glad to know Dad's home for tea for once. He knows you've got something special you want to tell him. But hurry up. There's some emergency at the police station tonight and he'll have to rush off there straight after tea.'

'Oh, if he's that busy, I won't worry him,' said Anne.

Peter, always curious, asked softly:

'A police emergency? What's it about, Mum – do you know?'

'You should ask Dad that, not me,' Mrs Miller told him.

She was about to go out of the hall, in the direction of the kitchen, when suddenly she turned.

'All I know is, it's got a very funny name. Operation Devil Cat,' she said.

13

Talk of the Devil Cat

Anne waited until halfway through tea before she asked her father about Operation Devil Cat. She had a feeling that he wouldn't be too keen to talk about it and she was right.

Detective Superintendent Miller started so violently that he dropped a fork, loaded with sausage, which had been well on its way to his mouth. It fell on to his plate from quite a height, and several baked beans shot across the table.

'Devil Cat?' he barked. 'Where did you hear that word?'

'I told the children that was the name of the operation you were on,' Mrs Miller confessed. 'What's wrong? Is there something secret about it?'

'It's only the most hush-hush job Fenton CID have ever had,' the Detective Superintendent growled. 'We're under strict orders not even to breathe the name of it to anyone outside the force – and that goes for wives and families too. I can't think where I slipped up.'

'You shouted it at the top of your voice just now when you were giving orders on the phone to someone in the CID,' Mrs Miller said. 'I couldn't help overhearing, and I told the children because it sounded such a funny name. I didn't realise that I was –'

'Letting the cat out of the bag, Mrs Miller?' drawled Barry.

Everybody laughed, except the Detective Superintendent, who glowered ferociously. But finally, even he grinned.

'Oh, well, I suppose not much harm's been done,' he said. 'Come midnight, the whole thing will be over anyway, and it won't matter much who knows about it. If you kids can be trusted to keep your traps shut until then –'

'Don't worry, Dad. Keeping things secret is our speciality,' said Anne. She tried to say it coolly, but thinking of Kate, she almost choked over the words.

'In any case, you haven't really told us anything, except the name,' said Peter. 'What is the Devil Cat?' Very quietly, his eyes suddenly narrowed, he went on: 'From all this fuss, anyone would think it was the code name for a top-secret weapon.'

Detective Superintendent Miller didn't drop a fork this time. But he gave a jump which showed quite clearly that Peter had hit the mark.

'I sometimes think you're the one with the uncanny powers in this family, not Kate,' he said. 'Since you've guessed the main thing, I might as well tell you the rest. Yes, the Devil Cat *is* a secret weapon – probably a new kind of missile – and the interesting thing about it is that it's entirely British. Even the Americans haven't been given the details yet. Just about every secret service in the world is after it, to say nothing of terrorist organisations who might be planning to hijack it. And – since there's only one Devil Cat in existence at the moment – it has to be surrounded by top security, everywhere it goes.'

'And it's coming here tonight?' asked Peter.

Mr Miller nodded.

'That's right. It's being driven by road from Portsmouth to a military aerodrome in the Midlands, and the route runs right through the centre of Fenton. It's my job to make sure that nothing happens to it while it's passing through our area. It's not an easy task, I can tell you. It'll be going down Rochester Road, and that means it'll be passing literally miles of empty warehouses. Any one of them could be hiding spies or terrorists, but I haven't the time or the men to go through them all. The only thing I can do is make sure we search the most likely places – and I'll have to be pretty quick about that. That darned Devil Cat is coming through between eleven and twelve, and it's nearly six now. I ought to get down to that station right away.'

He shot up from the table, leaving most of his sausages and beans untouched. A few seconds later, the Detectives heard the front door slam behind him.

Suddenly, they didn't feel much like food either. They were all remembering Gorodny's threat that if CID men came to search the warehouses where the machines were, Kate would 'die – instantly'. And they were big warehouses, right on the Rochester Road. Mr Miller might well consider them 'likely places' . . .

As soon as they'd helped to clear the plates away, and given a very hasty, fumbling hand with the washing up, the Detectives rushed upstairs for an urgent conference. They decided to hold it in Anne's room. This was the furthest room along the landing, and there was less risk of anything they said being overheard by Mrs Miller, if she started wandering about the house.

The moment they'd closed the door, Peter said: 'Well, we know a lot now that we didn't know before. We know what the Devil Cat is, and when it will be passing – between eleven and twelve tonight. We know, too, that they'll be driving it right by the warehouse, so it's obvious that Gorodny and his friends are all set to do something to it.'

'But what?' said Anne and Barry together.

Peter looked very grim. 'Your guess is as good as mine. And since they've brought in machines straight out of a sci fi comic, I don't think any of our guesses are going to be much good, do you?'

'I hope you're right,' said Barry quietly, 'because I don't dare to tell you mine.'

There was an odd silence, which soon became a terrifying one. Anne, Peter and Barry just stared at each other, their minds full of fearful possibilities.

'I know what you're thinking,' said Anne. 'The Devil Cat is probably a nuclear missile – and those machines *could* be designed to trigger it off, blow it up. In that case, the whole of Fenton might go up!'

'The whole of Fenton!' said Barry. 'You mean the whole of London.'

Anne swallowed hard and became very quiet. Peter was shaking his head.

'I shouldn't think *any* machine could do that,' he said. 'And if they could, Gorodny and Co would be blowing themselves up with the rest of us! But they may be trying to hi-jack the Devil Cat in some way. What way I can't imagine.'

Barry, for once, wasn't lounging against any wall. He was nervously pacing up and down the room.

'There's got to be something we can do to stop them,' he said.

Anne was sitting on the very edge of her bed, so tense that she could feel the mattress quivering beneath her.

'If – if only we knew where they've taken Kate,' she said.

'As a matter of fact,' said Peter, 'I think we *do* know that.'

He was leaning back in the chair beside the bed,

and appeared to be the coolest of the three – until one noticed how furiously he was fiddling with the cord of the light over Anne's bed. He had twisted it round his fingers so tightly that his knuckles were white. Suddenly, maddeningly, he started to jerk the light on and off, on and off.

'Gorodny said that Kate would die *instantly* if a CID man came near those warehouses. Right? Well, that could only happen if Kate was being kept prisoner on the spot, somewhere in the warehouse buildings. But with all those machines and everything around, it would take an SAS raid to get her out. Here, what . . .'

Anne had shot to her feet so fast it was as though she'd been sitting on a coiled spring. Suddenly she was the old Anne, the reckless, impulsive lover of action.

'How about the Dean Street Detectives putting on a raid?' she suggested.

Barry stopped pacing.

Peter dropped the light cord, and stood up. 'You don't mean –' Peter began.

'– that at last you've recovered your nerve, O fearless leader?' finished Barry.

Anne glowered at them as ferociously as her father would have done. 'I'd never lost it,' she snapped. 'It was just that I couldn't see that there was anything we could do. But I can now. I can see *exactly* what we can do.'

Before the others could get over their astonishment, she was striding purposefully towards the door. She was so excited about her idea that she forgot even to explain it. She just shouted over her shoulder the words Barry had wondered if he'd ever hear again.

'Let's go!'

14

Into Action

'Where exactly are we going?' Barry inquired, adding mildly: 'If it's not too rude to ask.'

It was two minutes later, and he, Peter and Anne were getting on their bicycles in the drive outside the Millers' garage. They had told Mrs Miller that they were going to see someone, but wouldn't be long. Though in fact, it was anyone's guess how long they'd be . . .

Anne at last outlined her plan.

'We're going to the warehouses – eventually,' she said. 'But it would be crazy to try and break in there like we did last night. They'd be ready for us this time. So my idea is to start by going round to the Pearsons. If we could persuade Phil's father to give us – or draw us – a plan of the warehouses and then lend us a complete set of keys, we could work out an attack that would take them completely by surprise.'

It was Barry who was taken by surprise. He gave a low whistle of admiration. 'That's brilliant, really brill,' he said. 'Once we see that plan, we ought to be able to figure out where they're keeping Kate, too. It wouldn't be in one of the main warehouses – more probably in a small room, an adjoining office or something like that. If the plan showed them all . . .'

Peter was beginning to be his old doubting self.

'There are a lot of snags in all this,' he said gloomily.

'How are we going to persuade Mr Pearson to give us these things? The spies have got both him and Phil into a state of terror, as far as I can make out.'

Anne folded her arms, and looked quite fierce –from what could be seen of her face in the fading light. 'In that case,' she said, 'we shall have to be more terrifying still.'

Peter frowned. 'Let's not forget his weak heart.'

Anne glowered. 'Let's not forget Kate. It's her we'll be rescuing – if my plan succeeds.' Suddenly she remembered she was supposed to be a democratic leader. 'Of course, if you're both against it – and I can't pretend that there aren't terrible risks –'

She obviously didn't expect any objections. She was on her bike now, and about to ride off down the drive. Doubtful though he was, Peter decided not to make difficulties.

'As long as you promise to keep well away from the machines this time, dear sister –'

'Don't worry, I will!' said Anne fervently. The memory of those silent bullets still made her shiver, and so did the prospect of encountering again those weird, space-age machines. But this wasn't the time to worry about things like that, she told herself. This wasn't the time to worry about anything except the danger to Kate – and maybe, yes, maybe even to the world . . .

'What about you, Barry? You're with us, aren't you?'

'With you? I'm ahead of you!' Barry said.

And suddenly, he was on his bike, streaking off down the drive and out into the road. In a second, Anne was off after him, with Peter just behind her.

The Dean Street Detectives – what was left of them – were on their way. To what all three of them knew was by far the most fateful – and dangerous – exploit of their career.

They had no trouble finding the Pearsons' address. Anne had already looked it up in her new clients' notebook.

'It's 14, Rochester Lane,' she said.

'Sounds as though it leads off Rochester Road,' said Peter. 'It may even back on to the warehouses. Mr Pearson's firm would want their caretaker to be on the spot, by day or by night.'

'Right,' said Anne. 'So Rochester Road, here we come again!'

It was almost dark by the time they reached it, but it was a clear night, and there was still a pinky-red afterglow from the sunset in the sky. It clashed weirdly with the orange from the street lamps, and bathed those miles of empty warehouses in a very peculiar light indeed: neither pink nor orange exactly, but something in between, which gave the Detectives the odd feeling that they arrived not just in a ghost town, but on a ghost planet. An endless stream of cars and lorries were, as usual, roaring by.

'I wonder when the police will stop them,' Peter said. 'They're bound to cut off all the traffic on the road long before midnight, as part of Operation Devil Cat.'

Barry braked his bike, and peered around him. He had to screw up his eyes to make out anything in this strange, sinister gloom. 'Can't see any sign of your father's men searching these warehouses,' he said.

'You're not likely to,' said Peter. 'There are hundreds of warehouses, after all, and they're only searching a few. The CID men may never come within miles of this stretch of the road.'

'For Kate's sake, let's hope they don't,' said Anne. Like Barry, she'd stopped her bike, and was peering about her with screwed-up eyes. 'Has anyone spotted Rochester Lane yet?'

'I told you,' said Peter patiently, 'it'll be alongside the Benholt Plastics warehouses. Wait until we come to them . . .'

The Detectives rode on, and presently were passing the actual scene of the previous night's adventures. There was the tin sign they'd hidden behind, now blown over on its side. There was the wire-mesh fence they'd climbed through, although the hole in it wasn't visible from the road. And there was the glassless telephone box, which Anne had used to ring the Pearsons. The box, they now noticed, was at the corner of a small side road named – Rochester Lane.

'If only we'd known the Pearsons lived so close,' said Anne, 'we wouldn't have rung them – we'd have gone round. I wonder if Mr Pearson would still have pretended that Phil was sick, and couldn't talk to us.'

'He'd have gone further than that,' said Peter. 'I bet he'd have pretended they were all out, and simply refused to answer the door. Come to think of it,' he added, as they turned their bikes into Rochester Lane, 'that's more than likely what he'll do right now!'

'In that case,' said Anne, 'we'll just have to keep ringing and knocking until they can't stand it any more.'

'He can't pretend there's nobody in tonight, anyway,' said Barry. 'That's number fourteen, isn't it? Well, there are lights on in the hall and lounge, and on the porch.'

'That wouldn't stop him,' said Peter. 'Lots of people leave lights on when they're out, because of burglars.'

They propped their bikes against the kerb, and a

moment later, were walking up the path of number fourteen – a small detached house standing well back from the road, and very close to the Benholt warehouses, one of which reared up immediately behind it.

When they reached the front door, Anne gave a sharp rat-tat on the knocker, waited for less than a second, and then jabbed hard at a bellpush beside the door. It looked as though, once again, Peter's guess was right. Even after ten rat-tats and as many rings, no one had come to the door.

Peter frowned. 'There's something odd about this,' he whispered.

'What do you mean – odd?' Anne whispered back. 'You predicted that they'd pretend to be out.'

'Ye-es,' said Peter. 'But they're pretending amazingly hard. I heard one faint gasp from somewhere when you first knocked – but since then, not a footstep or a whisper. It's as though all the Pearsons froze to the spot and haven't dared to move since then. If that isn't odd, what is?'

'They're just scared,' breathed Barry. Suddenly he had a vivid memory of how Phil had sounded on the phone that morning: hoarse and panting with naked fear crackling through every word. 'That man who called on them at dawn could obviously teach a few things to Dracula.'

'Well, they're not going to freeze to any spots when *we're* calling,' said Anne. 'This ought to thaw them out.'

She began knocking and ringing simultaneously, and kept on and on until finally, there were heavy plodding footsteps the other side, and Phil came to open the door.

He was *still* scared. That was obvious at a glance. His face was so flushed and beaded with sweat that he might have come straight out of a sauna. He was shaking, too – so violently that he could hardly grip the handle of the door.

'H-h-hullo,' he said. 'S-s-sorry, but I-I'm afraid I m-m-must ask you to g-go away.'

'Well, really!' said Anne.

'Now, Phil, my old mate,' drawled Barry, pushing him gently but firmly back into his own hall. 'I ask you, is that a nice way to treat friends? We haven't come to see you, anyway, but to have a few words with your father. Where *is* Mr Pearson?'

Phil was behaving even more oddly now. He seemed to be making strange signals, and it was almost as if he was trying to whisper some kind of warning. But he couldn't get the words out. His mouth just opened and shut like a goldfish's.

Peter was the only one who began to understand.

'Wait!' he whispered. 'I think he's telling us that . . .'

There was never any stopping Anne, though, when she was roused.

There was an open door the other side of the hall, obviously leading to the lounge. If Mr Pearson was anywhere, he would be there, she told herself. Pushing roughly past Phil, she walked straight through the open doorway. Barry and a protesting Peter followed behind.

Mr Pearson was there, all right. A thin, nervous-looking man in his shirtsleeves, with a face as red as his son's but startlingly thin, he was sitting in a deep armchair on one side of a fireplace. His wife, a plump, comfortable-looking woman in her middle forties, was in the armchair opposite. But both she and her husband were sitting oddly, bolt upright, as tense as though they were staring into the nozzle of a gun.

It didn't take the Detectives long to find out why.

A man with a revolver stepped out from behind the open door – and turned its nozzle on *them*.

'Hands up and don't move, any of you,' he said. 'Just copy the Pearsons here, and you'll be okay. If you try anything –'

He didn't complete the threat, but his eyes did. Cold and glittering, they were the most callous-looking that the Detectives had ever seen.

Clearly, this was the man who had come at dawn to frighten the Pearsons. And to make sure they remained frightened, he had obviously *stayed all day* . . .

15

The Gun on the Table

A lot of other things suddenly became clear to the Detectives. Barry needed no telling now why Phil had sounded so scared on the phone that morning. This man had probably had a gun in his back the whole time, and told him exactly what to say. It was equally obvious why Phil hadn't come into school that day, and why he and his parents were in such a state. Since dawn that morning – in other words, for thirteen or fourteen hours – they'd been doing everything under the threat of that gun: even the ordinary, everyday things like getting dressed, making beds, preparing food. The strain must have been terrible for all of them; and what it was doing to Mr Pearson's weak heart didn't bear thinking about.

For the next four hours – from seven until around eleven – the Detectives were forced to share that strain.

They'd thought at first that it would be easy to find a way of beating the terrorist and grabbing his gun. After all, including Phil and his parents, there were six of them against one. But the man was obviously highly trained or highly experienced or both, and didn't give anyone the slightest chance.

For one thing, he seemed to sense that the Detectives liked acting together, as a team – and made sure that they kept well apart from each other, even in the crowded living room. He made Anne sit on a chair by the door. Peter had to stand in a corner, like a naughty boy, except that he was allowed to face the room. Barry had to stand with his back to the bookcase – a glass-fronted one, so there was no chance of him seizing and hurling a book. Mr and Mrs Pearson were allowed to remain in their armchairs by the fire, but Phil was made to stand well away from them, with his back against a wall.

The living room had a dining area at one end, where there was a long mahogany table surrounded by chairs, with a bay window behind it. The man pulled out a chair, and seated himself behind the table, with his right hand – the one holding the revolver – resting on top of it. This was again a clever move on his part. From there, he could see everybody in the room, and anyone who tried to jump him and grab the gun would first have to climb over, or get round, that table. And he had made sure that no one was in a position even to try. Peter and Anne were at the opposite end of the room. Barry was near the right end of the table, and Phil quite near the left one; but it was a very long table, and that meant that they were each a good two metres away from the terrorist. To dive at him across all that mahogany – in the face of that loaded gun – they'd have to be total lunatics. In any case, Phil hardly looked the type to try anything at all. His face was still running with sweat, and he was trembling uncontrollably.

Minute after minute, and finally hour after hour, went by, without the situation changing in any way. Occasionally someone would make some kind of sound, or movement. Once Mr Pearson leaned back in his armchair, making it creak. Once Phil scratched himself nervously. Once Barry put his hands in his pockets.

Once Anne sighed heavily, and started to tap a foot against the floor.

Each time, exactly the same thing happened. The terrorist would instantly raise his arm off the table, and level the gun at the head of the person who'd made the noise. The safety catch would click back; his forefinger would whiten on the trigger.

'One more move,' he'd say, 'or one more sound out of you – and that will be *it*, my friend . . .'

And the look in his eyes would leave the mover, or sound-maker, in no doubt that he – or she – was within a split-second of death.

The Detectives had never felt so frustrated in their lives. Dozens and in the end hundreds of plans sped through their whirling brains. But they had to reject every single one of them as either too risky, or doomed to failure from the start. There was nothing they could do that wouldn't involve some kind of sound or movement – and that man's eyes and ears were sharp enough to detect the slightest. Spaced out as they were from each other, they couldn't even exchange whispers or signals.

No, Barry told himself for the thousandth time, they'd got to admit it. Up against a hardened pro who didn't miss a trick, even the Dean Street Detectives were as helpless as babes.

Or *were* they?

Suddenly the unbelievable happened. The terrorist's right hand must have started aching – not surprisingly, with all those hours of holding that revolver. He put the gun down on the table in front of him, and leaned back in his chair, yawning and stretching. Obviously he thought he'd got all the people in the room so terrified that he could relax and take a few risks at last.

Instantly, a brand new action plan – it seemed like the millionth of the night – was born in Barry's mind. He was near enough to the table to jump forward and get hold of one end of it. If he lifted the end high enough and fast enough, the table would tilt so sharply that the gun would slide away down to the other end before the terrorist could reach it.

Phil was at the far end. If he could grab the gun quickly enough –

Barry's spirits suddenly sank as fast as they had soared.

What was he thinking of? Phil wasn't a Detective. He was just a dim fat kid, with nerves of jelly and a brain to match . . .

Barry winced as he found himself thinking that. He, of all people, ought to know that fat boys weren't freaks; that often, in fact, they were frustrated heroes. Given a chance, Phil might do anything – though to look at him, sweating and quivering over there, no one would imagine it.

Barry caught Phil's eye and gave him a broad wink. Phil was so amazed that he started violently, the fool. Fortunately the gunman didn't notice it. He was still in the middle of that luxurious stretch. But he wouldn't be, much longer. Any second he'd be lowering his arms, reaching for the gun.

It was now or never, Barry told himself. And whether or not Phil messed the whole thing up, he *had* to have a go.

It was a moment before he could make himself move. Four hours of standing still had frozen his muscles; he had pins and needles in his right leg and one of his arms was numb.

Instead of the smooth, lightning leap he'd intended, all he could manage was a lumbering lurch forward.

It did its job, though. In a flash, he had grabbed the table. It turned out to be lighter than it looked, and in the same split second, he had tilted it to all of eighty degrees.

He even managed a joke, though it was not one of his brightest ones.

'Going . . . going . . . gun,' he murmured.

It described the situation, anyway. The terrorist's gun shot down the table faster than a cannoning snooker ball – straight into the pudgy hands of Phil Pearson, who dropped it on the floor.

'Oh, no!' Barry groaned. 'Grab it, Phil! Quick! *Point* it – '

The terrorist had got to his feet now, and was diving at the gun across the crazily tilted table. Barry hurriedly let go of his end. The table landed back on the floor with a resounding crash, jarring the terrorist's body from his head to his toes.

White and shaken now, the man staggered to his feet – to be rocked back on his heels by a totally unexpected sight.

Phil Pearson had picked up the gun, and was fumbling with it no longer. He was holding it rock steady, and levelling it with terrifying precision at the terrorist's heart. As the man stared dazedly, he clicked back the safety-catch, and his fat forefinger whitened on the trigger.

'One – one move,' he said, in a hoarse, but passable imitation of the other's voice, 'one move, and that will be *it*, my friend.'

The terrorist laughed scornfully. 'You know as well as I do you'll never fire that gun. Give it to me, or I'll – '

Phil had a good answer for that. He fired – wide, way over the gunman's head. The bullet smacked into the bookcase behind Barry. Slivers of glass showered on to the carpet with the force of small hailstones.

Mr Pearson shot out of his chair. 'Careful, son. You could *kill* someone with that thing.'

It was a typical fatherly interruption – but it proved disastrous.

Mr Pearson suddenly felt giddy and swayed. Mrs Pearson rushed to his side, shouting. And Phil wouldn't have been human if he hadn't looked round to see if his parents were okay.

That was all the terrorist needed. He turned and ran – straight at the bay window behind him. Barry tried to give chase, but the table was in his way. Before he could jump over it, the terrorist had sprung on to the sill, kicked out the nearest window, and disappeared into the darkness of the garden.

Barry was about to follow – but Anne stopped him.

'Let him go. We've got a lot to do tonight – remember? And hardly any time to do it in at all.'

She turned to Mr Pearson, who was back in his armchair, and asked him gently for a plan of the warehouses and the keys. He was still feeling groggy, but was well enough to nod, and to tell her where she'd find them.

As she went to fetch them, Mrs Pearson rushed off to get her husband some pills; Peter came stiffly out of his corner and started to congratulate Barry, and Phil just stared dazedly down at the gun, which was still smoking in his hand.

Barry waved aside Peter's congratulations and pointed at Phil.

'There's the boy who really turned the tables. All I did was – er – tilt one of them slightly.' Phil began to redden – and turned crimson as Barry asked him: 'What does it feel like to be the hero of the hour? I don't remember ever having that feeling – before I got myself thin.'

Phil gasped.

'Before – you – got – yourself – '

With a great effort, because he hated remembering those days, Barry admitted to Phil that he'd once been fatter than he was.

'Didn't take me long to slim down, though,' he finished. 'And it won't take you long, either, once I show you how. All part of our service to clients,' he added, and gently removed the gun from Phil's hand. He looked as though he was about to turn Western, and whoop and holler and fire it at the ceiling . . .

Anne was back now, with the chart and the keys of the warehouse. She spread the chart out on the carpet, and she, Peter and Barry started poring over it. It didn't take them long, either, to choose the ideal spot to begin operations. A small gate, marked 'Caretaker Only', led into the warehouse grounds from the end of the Pearsons' garden – not twenty metres from where they were now!

'They won't be expecting anyone to come in that way,' said Anne. 'They'll reckon we're all still being held up by that villain.'

'Not if he's rushed back there and raised the alarm,' said Barry.

'I don't think he's done that,' said Peter. 'I heard his car drive off just now – at ninety miles an hour, from the sound of it! I reckon he's terrified of admitting to his bosses that he was beaten by us, and is clearing off with all possible speed.'

'Which way did he go, did you notice?' asked Barry.

'Down the lane, *away* from Rochester Road,' said Peter. 'I think all the traffic on the road itself has been stopped by now. It's pretty near this house – yet I haven't heard a lorry going past for ages. Have either of you?'

All three Detectives stopped and listened. The whole area seemed to have become ominously quiet.

Anne looked at her watch, which said 11.13 and 10 seconds. And the Devil Cat was passing between eleven and twelve! If their raid was to have any chance, they'd better start it right away.

She borrowed a torch from Phil, who badly wanted to go with them. But his parents wouldn't hear of it. Mr Pearson didn't want any of them to go.

'You've no idea what danger you'll be walking into. Those machines –'

He broke off, breathless.

'Yes?' said Peter quietly. 'What about those machines, Mr Pearson? Do you, by any chance, know what they do?'

Mr Pearson tried to struggle up from his chair.

'They *spy*!' he said. 'On anything, anywhere, wherever it's hidden, they – they *spy* . . .'

That was all he could say. He fell back, blue in the face and gasping.

'Don't worry. He's had many worse turns than this.' said Mrs Pearson. 'He'll be all right – but please leave him alone.'

She and her son began to fuss over him, arranging cushions, putting up his feet. While this was going on, the Detectives quietly left the house by the back door, and found themselves in the Pearsons' garden. It was small, with just a patch of lawn and a few apple trees. There was no wall at the end of it – only the wire mesh fence of the warehouse compound. As the chart had shown, there was a small caretaker's gate set in the middle of this fence.

Anne went straight up to it and was trying to find

the key to fit the padlock when they heard a strange sound: a soft yet heavy rumbling, like distant thunder except that it wasn't distant, it was shaking the ground beneath their feet.

'What on earth's that?' breathed Barry.

'We'll soon know,' said Peter. 'It's coming from not very far beyond this gate.'

Anne had found the right key now, and the padlock sprang open in her hands.

She unlocked the gate, and one by one, the Detectives slipped through it. Then they gasped – and it was all they could do not to turn and run back into the garden.

They were standing on a concrete path running right round the perimeter of the warehouse compound, just inside the fence. It was not completely dark, because the lights in Rochester Road were near enough to spread their orange glow over the whole scene. And in that eerie gloom, the Detectives saw something even eerier.

Six of the strange, camera-like machines were coming along the path. There was no sign of anyone driving them, or being anywhere near them. They were moving entirely on their own, on small tyred wheels, the lenses in their camera 'heads' gleaming like huge, sinister, all-seeing eyes.

'Blimey!' said Barry. 'The Daleks are taking over. Lead me to the Tardis, quick!'

Neither Peter nor Anne felt like laughing. Anne was staring at those gleaming lenses as though hypnotised.

'You – you don't suppose they can see us?' she whispered.

'No, of course not,' said Peter hoarsely.

His words could hardly be heard above the rumbling as the machines came closer and closer. They were only about six metres away from them now, and the concrete beneath their feet was quivering almost as though they were in the middle of an earthquake.

'I hope you're right,' Barry shouted above the noise. He wasn't joking now. He was looking almost as hypnotised as Anne. 'Because I've a nasty feeling that – that we've had it if they can!'

16

The Creaking Shed

Peter, as usual, did prove to be right.

The machines, all six of them, simply trundled past the Detectives and went on their strange, softly rumbling and yet earthshaking way in the direction of the Rochester Road end of the warehouse compound. Suddenly they turned into one of the big warehouses. Once they were out of sight and out of earshot, the whole place returned to its usual 'ghost town' quiet.

Barry produced a handkerchief, and mopped his forehead.

'Well, that's quite enough sci fi for me for tonight. It only wanted one of those things to say "Good evening, intruders" and I'd have jumped high enough to clear that fence.'

Peter ran a hand through his hair, which felt sticky with sweat all over.

'Frankly, they had me worried for a moment too,' he said. 'But I can see now, they're not robots. They're just very heavy cameras on motorised wheels. Computer-programmed, probably, to follow a certain route when somebody presses the right button.'

'Then why do you suppose they're going down to the Rochester Road end now?' asked Barry. Then suddenly he answered his own question. 'Oh, of course. The Devil Cat is coming along there at almost any minute now.'

'Almost any minute!' Anne suddenly woke out of her near-trance. 'Hey, we've got to get moving. Where's that office where we figured they might be holding Kate?'

Peter, who was not only a good map-reader but a remarkable map-*rememberer*, pointed down the path.

'It should be down there, twelve metres along on the left.'

'We'd better be careful,' said Barry. 'It's bound to be guarded, if Kate *is* there. Though whether by humans, or more talking gadgets firing silent bullets –'

He broke off, as he heard Anne beside him give a little shudder. She hadn't forgotten – she would never forget – the horror of her near-escape from those bullets the night before. But she hadn't earned the nickname of 'fearless leader' for nothing. Remembering things like that wasn't the way to help Kate, she told herself – and was suddenly moving quickly and silently down the path, way ahead of Barry and Peter.

She reached the office first, and when they caught her up, was standing in the middle of the path with her arms folded, staring at it in dismay. It was nothing but an ancient, rusty Nissen hut, tucked in between two of the massive warehouses. No lights were on inside it. Its window panes were cracked and thick with grime. And the whole place looked so rickety that it seemed as though the slightest puff of wind would blow it over. Even as they stood there, odd creaks came from inside it, suggesting that something somewhere was about to give way.

'This can't be the place they're keeping Kate,' said Anne. 'It doesn't look as though anyone has been near it for years.'

'No one has been near *anything* here for years,' said Barry. 'These are disused warehouses, remember –

visited only by the caretaker and the odd spying machine. We might as well try the door.'

Anne tried it, and found that it was locked. She tried all the keys she'd brought with her, and the very last one fitted. The door creaked loudly as it opened.

'This way for Dracula Castle,' said Barry. 'Please pay the skeleton on the left as you enter.'

Anne was the first to go in, and squealed as the first floorboard she stepped on creaked even more loudly than the door. She felt for a light-switch, found one, and clicked it on. Rather to her surprise, a bare electric bulb flashed on overhead.

'Is that wise?' asked Peter anxiously. 'If somebody passing saw the light . . .'

He broke off, whistling softly. The scene in front of him drove everything else from his mind.

The shed was almost empty, except for an ancient office desk under one of the grimy windows, and a battered wooden cupboard on the far side. The rest was just an expanse of bare floorboards; but it was what was *on* those floorboards that set Peter's brain racing. They were strewn with objects – very odd objects, some of them. They included four bits of wood that had obviously been the legs of a plain wooden chair. Scattered amongst them were larger bits of wood that looked like other parts of the same chair – its seat and back, perhaps. Nearby were four or five short pieces of rope; a bit of cloth, clearly ripped from a blue Dean Street School skirt – and, finally, a shoe.

It was Anne, not Peter, who pounced on the shoe.

'That's Kate's,' she said instantly. 'I'd know it anywhere. So we guessed right. They *were* keeping her here.'

'With difficulty, I'd say,' said Peter. He was prowling furiously round the shed, picking up and peering at everything he came to. 'You know what we're looking at, don't you? The remains of a full-scale Murphy-style punch-up.'

Barry burst out laughing. 'Trust battling Kate to keep the Detectives' flag flying! What do you reckon happened?'

'That's easy,' said Peter. 'Kate was dragged in here and bound hand and foot to a wooden chair. A very rickety wooden chair, that had probably been rotting away in the shed for years. As Kate kicked and struggled, the chair must have simply fallen apart, setting her free. Obviously one of the guards heard the noise and came in. And Kate, I would guess, seized a chair-leg and started a battle royal. Then –'

He broke off, his face changing, and his eyes so narrow they were almost closed.

'Then what?' said Anne impatiently.

Peter had been examining one of the chair-legs when his expression had altered. Anne snatched it from him – and then her face changed too.

'Oh,' she gasped.

Once again, Barry found himself feeling out of it, never having had the Millers' detective experience.

'What *is* it?' he asked.

For answer, Peter held the chair-leg up to the light. For about the first ten centimetres, it was covered in blood.

'Either Kate nearly murdered somebody,' he said, 'or that somebody grabbed this leg and – and –'

His voice faltered, as he suddenly noticed something else. Sticking to the centre of the patch of blood was a long strand of hair. Bright *red* hair . . .

'And nearly murdered her,' he finished, letting the stick fall back on the floor.

It fell with a clatter, and after that there were no

more sounds, except for the non-stop creaks that seemed to be a part of this place.

Barry, Peter and Anne stared at each other, uncertain what to say or do. They were all wondering the same thing. Not where was Kate, but was Kate anywhere? She could so easily be lying somewhere, perhaps under these very floorboards, dead . . .

The silence dragged on, and became almost unbearable. So, suddenly, did that irritating *creak, creak, creak . . . creak, creak, creak . . . creak, creak, creak.*

Until Peter, his eyes suddenly wide-open and blazing with excitement, shouted:

'Those creaks. They're coming from the cupboard. And they're signalling. Don't you hear? They're regular, not accidental. So I don't think there's much doubt who's making them.'

17

The Spying Machines

The Detectives rushed to the battered cupboard on the far side of the room. Barry reached it first, and opened the door. He stepped back, startled, at what he saw.

Kate was lying at the bottom of the cupboard, and looked in a bad way. Her hands and feet were tied, and she had been gagged so tightly, with her own school scarf – that her eyes, above it, seemed to be popping out of her head. She had been so cramped down there that there had been no room to draw her feet back and kick against the door. But like everything else in the shed, the cupboard was so rickety that she only had to lean hard against one of its sides to make it creak.

It took Barry and Anne, between them, only a few seconds to pull her out and take off the ropes and scarf. A couple of handkerchiefs had been stuffed in her mouth to make sure she made no sound. She spat them out so fast that they shot out of her mouth like bullets.

'Urrrrrghhhhh!' she yelped. 'It does terrible things to your tonsils, trying to scream with half a dozen handkerchiefs stuffed down your throat. I've not been enjoying myself, I'm telling you, not been enjoying myself at all.'

'Neither have the villains, from the look of things,' said Barry, imitating her Irish accent. ''Tis a splendid fight you put up, Katie me darling – that's plain for all to see.'

Kate's eyes weren't popping out now. They were blazing with the old Murphy fury. 'Oh, I cracked a few heads with a chair-leg. Serve 'em right for tying me to the hardest, rottenest old wooden chair in all the world. But what was the good of that? I'd forgotten that a collapsing chair sends *four* legs across the room. Someone grabbed one of those other legs, crept up behind me – and the next thing I knew I was knowing nothing at all, because everything had gone black. When I came to, everything was still black – because there I was, trussed up like a chicken in that pokey hole of a cupboard. I thought I was a goner, I tell you. And when I heard you three come in, and realised I couldn't make a sound except a tiny creaking – '

She didn't look so much like a battling Murphy now. She had touched her hair, and found that a bit of it was matted with dried blood. She swallowed hard, and looked just for a moment as if she was going to faint.

'Who *is* this man who keeps creeping up behind me and bashing me on the back of my poor head? It's happened twice to me today. Once in the – the corridor of ghosts, and now here in this room. I never see him. I can't guess who he is.' Her face was white now, and haunted-looking. 'I – I just hear his footsteps, at the very last moment, when it's too late even to turn . . .'

Anne's eyes were blazing now, almost an angrily as Kate's. 'We can guess who he is all right,' she said. 'Peter found his footprints behind yours in the corridor. It's our old, old friend, Gorodny.'

'Gorodny!' Kate recovered abruptly. 'Why, that evil little man! I always knew he was a creep.' Suddenly the whole strangeness of the situation dawned on her, and started an explosion of questions. 'But what was Gorodny doing here? Come to that, what are you all doing here? And if it's not too much to ask, where are we?'

Anne hurriedly explained all that had happened. But if she thought that would stop Kate asking questions, she was wrong. Screwing up her freckled face, she immediately asked the most important question of the night.

'So these cameras on wheels have taken to moving around like Daleks,' she said. 'That's very interesting – but I still don't get it. They're only cameras after all. How can they capture a secret weapon coming along the road outside on a thundering juggernaut of a lorry?'

Peter started violently.

'Of course!' he shouted. 'You've said it, Kate! There's only one way that cameras can capture anything. By *photographing* it!'

Suddenly he was pacing the shed, the floorboards beneath his feet giving out loud creaks with every step. 'We know that these are very advanced machines. They can photograph in the dark. They have infra-red rays or laser beams that can even take a photo of a face through a mask. Well, then. Maybe they can do a lot more. Maybe, if they can be brought alongside the Devil Cat as it passes, they can photograph it straight through a warehouse wall, and even through the side of a lorry. Perhaps those rays can even go through the metal casing of the weapon itself and photograph the whole thing *right to the core*! You may think I'm talking science fiction – but after all, if the core is glowing, or radioactive . . .'

Barry was becoming excited too.

'I don't think you're talking science fiction at all,'

he said. 'This fits in pretty well with what Mr Pearson said about the machines. "On anything, anywhere, wherever it's hidden – they spy." Strewth! Gadgets like these must make it an easy life for secret agents these days. All they've had to do is discover which route the Devil Cat is taking. Then they simply find a disused warehouse or two along the route; move in these cameras, out of sight behind a warehouse wall– and then, *click*! suddenly Britain's top secret isn't secret any more. No one on our side would be any the wiser. They'd never dream anything like this could happen, and would carry on thinking that their secret was still absolutely safe. You've got to admit, the whole scheme is brilliant, from their point of view.'

Barry was carried away by his own enthusiasm. 'The machines are pretty brilliant too. They can defend themselves if they're spied on. And no one has to hump them about – they're computer-programmed to move just when and where they're told. I suppose what we saw just now was some of them moving up into the front line, so to speak. They must have gone into a warehouse with a wall running right alongside Rochester Road. Either their rays can penetrate that wall, or special spyholes have been drilled into the corrugated iron for them to use. And as soon as the Devil Cat passes . . .'

Anne suddenly sprang into action.

'It's *not* going to pass! It's not going to come near this place, if we can help it. There must be people out in Rochester Road now – the police cordoning off the area, CID men standing by. Probably Dad's somewhere around himself. We've got to get out there and contact someone – quick.'

Peter stopped pacing and frowned.

'Rochester Road goes on for miles. There may not

be anyone in this particular stretch of it at all. And there are bound to be agents watching the main gate. Why don't we sneak out the way we came in, through the caretaker's gate and call Dad from the Pearsons' phone? Even if he's around here, in a CID car, they could contact him by radio –'

'That makes sense to me,' said Barry.

'And to me,' said Kate. 'What are we waiting for?'

It certainly wasn't for Anne, who was already half-way across to the door, her feet making as noisy creaks as Peter's had done. Suddenly, though, there was a creak that didn't come from the boards. A long, 'Dracula's-castle' creak that could only mean one thing – and which froze them all to the spot, staring at the slowly-opening door.

The next moment, for the second time that evening, the Detectives were being ordered not to move, and were facing the nozzle of a gun.

This time, though, there were differences.

The gun was unlike anything that they had ever seen. It was in the shape of a metal globe, about half the size of a goldfish bowl, and obviously belonged to this strange, 007 world of X-ray cameras and soundless bullets.

It was terrifying to think what might happen if its odd, bulbous trigger was pressed. And the man behind the gun did not look as if he would hesitate to press it – although it might make his watery eyes fill with tears.

It was Mr George Gorodny.

18

Mr Gorodny Weeps

It was obvious that Mr Gorodny had been up to his old tricks, and had been listening outside the door. He seemed to know everything the Detectives had been saying.

'I realise now why my instructions were to watch you good,' he told them. 'You have guessed so much of the truth about our machines. You are certainly exceptional children. If I were really a teacher, I would be proud to have you in my class. But I am not a teacher. I am an enemy with orders to eliminate all dangers . . . and I am sorry to say that you have become very dangerous indeed . . .'

He had moved right into the shed now, and was standing, blinking mildly in the light, and staring round at them with an expression of great sadness. It was as though he was on the point of deciding that it was his duty to kill them all, there and then.

'We'll see about that,' thought Barry, and was on the point of jumping him. Out of the corners of his eyes, he could see Anne tensing, and knew that she had the same idea. Only one thing made them hesitate. It was so difficult to know what they were up against – what that strange global gun would do. Would it fire one bullet – or a stream of them?

A stream, probably, Anne guessed – and she imagined that the globe-like shape was to cut all noise.

It was a terrifying thought, but as like as not, that thing could wipe out all of them, in seconds, without a sound being heard outside the shed.

Still, if she and Barry pounced together, from different angles, so that Gorodny got confused, and didn't know which of them to aim at, there was just a chance that –

Peter, meanwhile, was working on a plan of his own.

Supposing Gorodny's weeping in front of so many classes hadn't been just an act? Supposing he really did suffer from some kind of nervous tension, which affected his eyes? It hadn't troubled him when he had rescued Barry from a classful of skinheads. But perhaps other things started it off – like noises coming from all directions. In which case, what they had to do was keep him talking and wait for a chance to experiment.

'Mr G-gorodny,' he said suddenly. Keeping up a conversation with a villain brandishing a gun wasn't really in Peter's line. His voice sounded hoarse and shakey. But the words came out clearly enough to make Gorodny jump.

'Yes, Peter?'

'Our – our guesses about the machines. You say they were absolutely right?'

Gorodny smiled. His eyes behind those thick glasses actually gleamed. He was obviously very proud of those machines. Perhaps he had played a part in developing them. He looked more like a technologist than a schoolteacher – or, for that matter, a spy.

'Yes, yes. As I told you – you guessed good. The machines *are* cameras equipped with high-intensity laser beams, and also heat sensors. They will be able to photograph every part of the Devil Cat, no matter how thick the casing around it!'

'But why do you need so many of them?'

'Because a modern weapon is a very intricate thing, and many pictures are needed, from many angles, to reveal all its secrets! And there is something else, something that you could not guess. The cameras are also radio transmitters. One split-second after they have photographed the weapon, the image will be flashed to a waiting van ten miles away. From there it will be beamed, via a network of secret transmitters, straight to my country. In other words, a moment after the Devil Cat passes these warehouses, every detail of it will be received on the other side of Europe – literally as fast as the speed of light! So maybe . . .' Mr Gorodny's face lost its sad expression. 'So maybe you are not so very dangerous to us as I thought. All I have to do is keep you here for a few minutes – until I hear that big Devil Cat lorry rumbling by – and *zut*! It will be all over. The secret will be ours – and nothing you or the police or the whole of British Intelligence can do will prevent it! That is good news for you, my friends.'

'Good news for *us*?' said Peter.

'Yes. It means that, if you remain still for just a few minutes, there is a chance that I will be allowed to let you live. You will be kept here, of course, until we have moved the machines away and closed down the whole operation. But then, I hope and pray that I shall be permitted to let you go. I am not a violent man, you see. All violence – especially violence against children – hurts me deep.'

Kate had, so far, kept very quiet. But this was altogether too much. Her head still ached all over from Gorodny's two blows. Suddenly she just saw red, and before she realised what she was doing, had picked up a chair-leg and started to walk forwards.

'This,' she shouted, 'is going to hurt you *very* deep, you creep!'

She broke off, stopped before she'd taken a step by that global gun. Gorodny had raised it, and was levelling it at the centre of her forehead.

'I will give you,' he said, 'just two seconds to drop that stick. *One* . . .'

Kate didn't wait for 'Two.' And she didn't exactly drop the chair-leg. She hurled it angrily on to the floorboards at her feet. It fell with a clatter, and rolled noisily across the boards.

Gorodny jumped. 'You stupid child. Are you trying to *make* me shoot?'

He licked his lips nervously. The gun in his hand was shaking. And his eyes, Peter noticed, had started watering.

Very, very cautiously, Peter trod on a loose floorboard that he knew was just in front of him. It gave out a soft, menacing creak. Barry, who was always very quick to catch on to anything, leaned hard against the cupboard door, which happened to be quite close behind him. It closed with a loud thud.

'Stop that!' shouted Gorodny, and suddenly he was screaming exactly as he had done in his first lesson with 4G. 'Quiet – please, I beg of you . . .'

His eyes were watering badly now . . . and they flooded with tears as Anne on one side of him, and Peter on the other, started a deafening duet with creaking floorboards – and Barry backed them up with more thuds on the cupboard door.

Nearly hysterical, and blinded by his tears, Gorodny pressed the bulbous trigger. The globe twitched eerily in his hand, and four bullets came spurting from its nozzle, without the slightest sound. But his aim was far too low. The bullets zipped into the floorboards –

which gave out four more deafening creaks, from four different parts of the room.

Gorodny was now pleading pitiably.

'Stop it – I can't – can't *stand* this creaking . . .'

In point of fact, he only heard one creak more. It was the creak of Kate's footsteps, immediately behind him.

Then that chair-leg landed on the back of his head, and, as Kate would have put it, the next thing he knew, he was knowing nothing.

19

Collision Course

Barry prised the global gun out of the hand of the unconscious Gorodny.

'This'll give our raid a real SAS touch,' he said, and looked round at the others. 'Where do we go now? Back to the Pearsons' or is it too late for phoning?'

'I'm afraid,' said Peter. 'it's too late for *anything*! Listen.'

From the direction of Rochester Road came the roar of an approaching motorcade. They could hear at least four motor-cycles, sundry cars and behind it all, the massive rumble of an enormous transporter. The sound was so loud it was obvious that the first vehicles of the procession were about to pass the main gate. It wouldn't be more than a few seconds after that before the transporter itself was rumbling past, with its top-secret cargo.

The thought of that – and the barrage of super-cameras waiting to click, waiting to flash the secret halfway across the globe at the speed of light – made the Detectives move pretty fast themselves. In half a second they were running – harder than they had ever run in their lives – down a concrete path towards the Rochester Road end of the warehouse compound. Only Kate had stolen a quick glance back at the silent and still Gorodny. Her anger had gone now. She was praying she hadn't seriously injured him. At least there was no blood on his hair, as there was on hers . . .

None of the others had any thoughts to spare for Gorodny. Way ahead of them – a hopelessly long way, it seemed – they could see the main gate, surrounded by the wire mesh. And through the gate, they could glimpse the motor-cycles roaring past, the helmets of their uniformed drivers glittering in the orange light.

'Obviously from some Army corps,' panted Peter. 'There's a badge on those helmets – did you see?'

No one replied. They were all too busy running – and battling against a mounting sense of helplessness and despair. They were still quite some distance away from those gates, and the motor-cyclists were already gone. A jeep-like vehicle was passing now, with Army officers in the rear. High-up officers, to judge from the red on their caps. The Devil Cat wouldn't be far behind them.

Anne's lungs felt as though they were nearly bursting, and so did her brain, as she struggled desperately to think and run at the same time. 'Let's – let's get one thing straight,' she gasped. 'Those cameras – they turned into a warehouse, didn't they? Now just which warehouse was it?'

'The one running alongside the road, to the right of the main gates,' Peter panted. 'They're probably lined up against that warehouse's wall. It faces the road, and the Cat will pass only about five metres in front of them.'

Anne struggled even harder to think, even though she knew she was losing speed in the process. 'The warehouse is on the right of the gates, you say. Well, the procession's coming from the left. So if we can stop the Devil Cat dead, right outside the main gate, it won't pass by those cameras, and it'll be safe!'

'Quite right, fearless leader,' said Barry. Even when

breathless, he could still sound mocking. 'But just how do we do that?'

'We could all shout together, at the tops of our voices,' said Kate.

'Even your voice, Katie me darling, would hardly carry hundreds of metres, above the roar of lorries and jeeps and motor-cycles,' said Barry.

Kate was never easily beaten. 'Well, then, you could use that globe thing to send silent bullets through its windscreen.'

Barry was losing patience. 'Don't be so ruddy silly! You'd need a high-velocity rifle to do that, from this distance. And even then, it might not stop – it'd be more likely to double its speed! Let's face it. Short of a miracle, there's absolutely nothing we can – My God!'

He stopped dead in his tracks, so abruptly that both Peter and Kate, who were bringing up the rear, cannoned into him, and they all three fell sprawling. Anne was also taken by surprise. She ran on a few paces before she realised what had happened. She turned and ran back, furiously angry.

'What are you playing at, for Heaven's sake? We haven't a split second to lose!'

'No. And now we needn't lose any! Look!'

Barry scrambled to his feet, and pointed. Hidden on the right, in the deep shadows between two warehouses, was a lorry, waiting with its cab door open and engine running. Obviously the agents were prepared for a quick getaway in case anything went wrong.

'You're crazy!' yelled Kate as Barry rushed towards that open door. 'You don't know how to drive. None of us do –'

But Barry was already climbing behind the wheel, and Anne was jumping into the cab beside him. Kate and Peter didn't argue. None of the Detectives ever did, in an extreme emergency. They had a strange talent, when it came to the point, for acting as one. In a flash, they were all side by side in the cab, and Kate, on the far left, was trying to slam the door.

It wasn't easy. A fierce-looking bearded giant had sprung out of the darkness of the alley, leaped on to the running board, and grabbed the outside handle.

'What the hell do you flaming kids think you're –'

He broke off, his mouth gaping as Barry pressed the trigger of the global gun and a stream of bullets shot past his ear. Trying to duck, he lost his footing on the running board and fell heavily on to the road.

Kate slammed the door hard. Two of the bullets had slammed through its window, and bits of glass cascaded all over her. She hardly noticed that. She could hear footsteps coming from several directions. The one thing that mattered was that they should get out of here – fast.

'Let's go!' she yelled, unintentionally imitating Anne. 'Let's go! Let's go! Let's GO!'

'I'm doing my best,' said Barry.

He knew how to start a car – he had seen Mr Bigley do it at least a hundred thousand times, and had sometimes practised the movements in his father's car – but lorries were different. He had found the clutch pedal, and was pressing it. He had found the hand-brake, which seemed an enormous distance away to his left, and had yanked that. He had found the headlamps button, and had pressed it. But what came next? For a moment, his mind was blank.

'The gear,' said Peter tensely. 'That lever. *There . . .*'

'Ah, yes. Thanks,' said Barry, and pulled it forward.

'Now the clutch,' said Anne, suddenly shouting. 'Quick. *Take your foot off the clutch* –'

Barry obeyed; Anne pressed her own foot hard on the accelerator, and suddenly the lorry was roaring, shuddering and lurching forward. The corrugated iron wall of a warehouse opposite leaped towards them, and came so close that it filled the windscreen, blindingly bright in the headlamps' glare. In the very nick of time, Barry swung the wheel and they turned right, out of the alley and down the concrete road to the main gates.

'Great driving,' yelled Kate, adding sourly: 'If we were on the bumper cars at Butlin's!'

Barry didn't answer. He was too busy shouting at Anne.

'Don't accelerate like that. Look at the speedometer, for Pete's sake. We're going much too fast!'

Anne took her foot off the accelerator – but it was too late. The distance between them and the main gates had shortened, in a flash, to fifty metres, forty– thirty – twenty –

In a sudden panic, Barry jammed on the handbrake, the footbrake, everything in sight. The lorry shivered all over, as though it was in high fever. The locked tyres screeched deafeningly.

But they still kept rushing on.

The main gates came leaping towards them, just as the warehouse wall had done. Through the wire mesh on either side of it, they could see every detail of the road beyond.

There, in the brilliant orange light, was a huge articulated lorry. And there, just ahead of it, was a police car, with someone very familiar in the back seat.

'Oh, no!' breathed Anne. 'I just don't believe it . . .'

They were on a non-stop collision course with the gates, the Devil Cat – and Detective Superintendent Miller!

20

The Devil Cat Passes

They hit the gates with a crash that shattered the windscreen. The gates themselves, fortunately relatively flimsy contraptions, flattened themselves across the road beyond with resounding clangs that shook the ground and raised thick clouds of dust: strange orange dust in the light of the street lamps. The drivers of the police car and the Devil Cat lorry braked frantically. The bonnet of the police car vanished under a mass of buckling metal. And the whole scene vanished as far as the Detectives were concerned. Nothing could be seen through the shattered windscreen and the dust except a vivid orange blur. All they could hear was screeching brakes – from the Devil Cat lorry, the police car, and the tortured tyres beneath their own feet. All they knew was that their lorry was still moving, still plunging on through the chaos and debris, and that it would be a miracle if it didn't hit something – or someone – soon . . .

Barry struggled desperately to turn the wheel and swing the lorry off its collision course. But sweat was streaming from every pore, and his hands were so sticky that they could scarcely get a grip. Then Anne leant over and grabbed the wheel herself – and by a panicky combined effort, she and Barry managed somehow to turn it all the way to the right.

The next moment, every thing went crazy, like a film taken by a cinecamera that was being tossed downstairs. With a shuddering rumble, the lorry crashed across the fallen gates, lurched out into the road, and swung right at such a dangerous angle that all the wheels on its left-hand side rose high in the air.

The Detectives found themselves sliding across the tilted driving cab like that gun on the Pearsons' table. All four of them ended in a helpless pile-up behind the wheel, jammed together so tight that driving was impossible. Everything, in fact, was impossible . . . except praying.

Then, suddenly, the crisis was over.

The lorry righted itself with a jolt that jarred every bone in their bodies – and came to a slow, quivering halt.

The dust was clearing now. Through the side windows they could see a crowd of people rushing towards them: motor-cyclists, policemen, army officers – and, in the forefront, a white-faced, furious-looking Detective Superintendent Miller.

'Something tells me we're not popular,' said Barry, shakily, as soon as he had got his breath.

'Well, we ruddy well ought to be,' said Anne. 'Look at the Devil Cat.'

The huge lorry carrying the mysterious weapon hadn't been so much as scratched. And it had been halted well out of range of the warehouse with the cameras.

Thanks to the Dean Street Detectives, Britain's top secret was a secret still.

Not that thanks was exactly what the Detectives received, when they opened the door of the driving cab and climbed shakily down into the road.

'I always said you'd nearly get yourselves killed one of these days,' roared Mr Miller. 'But you've surpassed yourselves this time. You nearly killed *me* into the bargain!'

An army officer came marching up. There was red all over his cap, and Peter suspected he was at least a brigadier, perhaps even a general.

'These children friends of yours, Superintendent? That's unfortunate. Because I'm placing them under military arrest – immediately!'

He barked orders, and soldiers surrounded the Detectives. They had unfamiliar uniforms. Barry wasn't sure, but they might have been SAS men.

Mr Miller tried to come to their rescue.

'Just a minute, Brigadier,' he growled. 'Surely you might hear what the children have to say first. There's bound to be *some* sort of explanation for all this . . .'

The Brigadier glared at the Detectives, as though he'd really like to put them in front of a firing squad without delay.

'An explanation?' he said. 'Very well. I'll listen.'

He didn't listen long. As soon as Anne had mentioned spying machines that could photograph through walls, and Barry had started to describe silent bullets, he stopped them with a contemptuous snort.

'I've never heard such imbecile rubbish in my life!' he roared. 'Take these children off and keep a close watch on them, while we clear up the mess they've made. Then I'll deal with them – and by Heaven, they've a lot to answer for!' He suddenly noticed the global gun, which Barry had brought with him out of the driving cab. 'Oh, and you'd better confiscate that stupid boy's space toy. He's a dangerous vandal. It might explode or something.'

Before Barry could so much as blink, the gun had been snatched from his hands, and he and the other

Detectives were being lined up, ready to be marched away.

'Sorry about this,' muttered Mr Miller. 'But Operation Devil Cat's under military intelligence. You're in their hands now, and there's nothing I can do.'

'Don't worry, Dad,' Anne whispered back. 'There's plenty *we* can do.' In a slightly louder whisper, she said to the others: 'Let's go!'

The soldiers imagined they were dealing with ordinary children. They simply weren't prepared for a full-scale Dean Street Detective operation – and were taken totally by surprise when the four simply shot through their legs, and streaked towards the gap in the wire mesh left by the fallen main gates.

'After them!' roared the Brigadier.

The SAS men, if that was what they were, hurled themselves across the road, and rushed through the hole in the mesh, into the darkness of the warehouse compound. The Brigadier followed at a more sedate pace, swinging a silver-mounted cane. Mr Miller strode grimly along beside him, fearful about what was going to happen now. A couple of captains and a lieutenant, as well as sundry policemen, brought up the rear.

The soldiers caught up with the Detectives just as they were entering the warehouse where the spying machines were. The machines could be glimpsed through the darkness, a whole row of them; but the soldiers weren't looking in that direction. They pounced on the Detectives, and suddenly Anne, Peter, Kate and Barry found themselves with their arms behind their backs, being held in an expert Commando grip. Kate didn't like that at all.

'Let me go, you – you *buffoons*!' she yelled. 'If you had any brains or eyes in your heads at all, you'd see that your real enemies are those crazy camera contraptions over there.'

The men paid no attention. Nor did the Brigadier, who was now arriving on the scene, with Mr Miller and the others. Nor did anyone else – until something (perhaps the Brigadier's swinging cane) interrupted an invisible electronic beam.

Immediately, a voice came booming out of the darkness – a voice that no one could ignore.

'*Good evening, intruders . . . Don't move an inch for ten seconds, or you will never intrude again.*'

The Brigadier's jaw dropped – and so did his silver-mounted cane. That evidently counted as a move. Bullets from a strangely silent source came whistling past his ears.

As soon as he could speak, he started barking orders – completely new orders.

'Get back, everybody. Let these children go – at once. And from now on, let's listen very carefully to what they say . . .'

It was an hour and a half later.

Under the Brigadier and Detective Superintendent Miller, the army and the police had carried out a full-scale search of the warehouses. Ten foreign agents had been arrested, including Gorodny, who had returned to consciousness just in time to be handcuffed and led away with the rest. Sixteen spying machines had been discovered, and earmarked for examination by MI6, the counter-espionage department of British Intelligence. Rochester Road had been cleared of the wrecked lorry, the smashed police car and the fallen gates, and the way was now open for the Devil Cat to resume its journey.

Another police car had been provided for Detective

Superintendent Miller, and he was waiting in it, with four sleepy Detectives beside him, to see the Cat finally on its way before they all went home to bed.

'It's just moving off now,' he told them. 'Just to be on the safe side, you'd better all close your eyes as it goes past. Outsiders aren't really supposed to come as close to it as this. After all, it *is* a top secret weapon.'

Anne started to point out that if it hadn't been for the Detectives, it wouldn't be a secret by now at all. But the roaring of the giant transporter starting up drowned her voice.

She looked at the others and winked. They all dutifully closed their eyes – for precisely two seconds. Then, to Mr Miller's horror, they suddenly bounded to their feet, waving and shouting at the tops of their voices.

'Good luck, pussy!' yelled the Dean Street Detectives as the Devil Cat finally passed by, thundering on its mysterious way through the orangey blackness of the night.